Consider the Octopus

Consider the Octopus

Nora Raleigh Baskin
AND *Gae Polisner*

GODWINBOOKS

HENRY HOLT AND COMPANY
NEW YORK

We only get one earth and a few oceans.
Thank you to all, especially the children,
who step up to keep them clean and safe.

Henry Holt and Company, *Publishers since 1866*
Henry Holt® is a registered trademark of Macmillan Publishing Group, LLC
120 Broadway, New York, NY 10271 ✦ mackids.com

Our books may be purchased in bulk for promotional, educational, or business
use. Please contact your local bookseller or the Macmillan Corporate and
Premium Sales Department at (800) 221-7945 ext. 5442 or by email at
MacmillanSpecialMarkets@macmillan.com.

Library of Congress Cataloging-in-Publication Data
Names: Baskin, Nora Raleigh, author. | Polisner, Gae, author.
Title: Consider the octopus / Nora Raleigh Baskin and Gae Polisner.
Description: First edition. | New York : Henry Holt and Company, 2022. |
    Audience: Ages 8–12. | Audience: Grades 4–6. | Summary: Told in alternating
    voices, twelve-year-olds JB Barnes and Sidney Miller meet aboard a scientific
    research ship after JB is tasked to invite a renowned scientist named Sidney Miller
    and mistakenly invites a girl with the same name who will do anything to get out of
    going to summer camp.
Identifiers: LCCN 2021030133 | ISBN 9781250793515 (hardcover)
Subjects: CYAC: Impersonation—Fiction. | Friendship—Fiction. |
    Water—Pollution—Fiction. | Ocean—Fiction.
Classification: LCC PZ7.B29233 Co 2022 | DDC [Fic]—dc23
LC record available at https://lccn.loc.gov/2021030133

First edition, 2022
Book design by Mallory Grigg
Emoji design by Lili Qian
Printed in the United States of America by Lakeside Book Company,
Harrisonburg, Virginia

10 9 8 7 6 5 4 3 2 1

I am here to say, our house is on fire . . .
I want you to act as you would in a crisis.

—GRETA THUNBERG, 16

The day science begins to study non-
physical phenomena, it will make more
progress in one decade than in all the
previous centuries of its existence.

—NIKOLA TESLA, DEAD

NOW

1.

JEREMY JB "FACE OF THE *OCEANIA II*" BARNES

The Mylar balloons, tied tight to the metal leg of the folding registration table, twist and glitter in the sweltering sunshine, waiting for me to come bake next to them. Earlier, Marco and Randi had argued over them, him saying, "Balloons are festive and make it easier to find us, plus fine for the environment so long as we cut them in half and recycle them properly afterward," and her saying, "Fine, if you don't mind being a total hypocrite and part of the bigger problem. Besides, how hard is it to spot two registration tables in front of a ginormous research ship docked only a quarter mile off that says *Oceania II* in white across its whole green side?"

Marco had won, per usual, by making an "executive decision," leaving Randi to glare at him. Now, I sit down next to the balloons on a wobbly folding chair and wait for the science-geek SEAmester kids to show up so I can start my super-important job of checking them in.

A mere two weeks ago, I would never have been given this "Face of the *Oceania II*" assignment, even in an emergency, so maybe Mom is right. Maybe the "fresh air and thinking time" are starting to rub off on me.

Not that me doing this job was exactly everyone's first choice. Marco was supposed to do it, but there was some sort of emergency, "all hands on deck," which meant Marco and Randi and Vance and even Sabira had to stay on board, which left only Henry and me to check everyone in, and since Henry can obviously schmooze better than I can about fancy science things, that put him in charge of the scientists, and me, checking in the SEAmester kids.

"If you're sure you can handle that . . . ?" Mom had asked, her words sounding more worried than like a big vote of confidence. Plus, she rumpled my hair, which isn't really something you should do if you want someone to feel fully competent. Besides, hadn't I just proved myself? Hadn't I located ten of the eighteen hard-to-find scientists from all over the globe? You think it's easy to tell a marine biologist from a climate biologist from a climatologist when they all have the same first name? Okay, well, at least two of them did.

But this guy here? He did it! And got ten—ten!—of the eighteen "hopefuls" on Captain Jim's invite list, from Zhang Liu to Samara Redmond to Dr. Sidney Miller from the Marine Lab at the Monterey Bay Aquarium, to RSVP they were coming.

I shift in my spot, glance at Henry still setting up his registration table, and then at the small brick building across the empty dock where ferry tickets are sold, wondering if I have time to run in and take a leak, but I can see cars beginning to pull in through the arrival zone, plus a shuttle bus, and I don't want to mess up by not being here to greet the first kids to arrive.

SIDNEY MILLER

Nana's fifteen-year-old pumpkin-orange Subaru station wagon looks right at home in the parking lot of the Seattle Food Co-op Warehouse. In fact, five spots down from where we are sitting in our car, there's another one almost identical, except that one has more bumper stickers. I know, right? Pretty hard to imagine.

But there it is.

"See," Nana says, pointing to the orange twin car. "Even the same dent on the passenger door. Now how do you explain that?"

I bet there are a ton of algorithms that could explain it. Starting with the number of orange Subaru station wagons sold in any given year. Like the demographic of people who purchased Subarus, in relation to those living in the Seattle area, and then the number of those same people who kept their car for ten years or more. I don't necessarily know the math to figure that all out, but I know there is some.

At the same time, how can I ignore coincidences like that ever again? I mean, it's what brought me here in the first place. That's exactly the reason I am about to attempt to sneak onto a ship and sail out into the Pacific Ocean for seven days. *The reason?* A ring toss game, a nail polish color, a goldfish, and what may possibly be nothing more than a simple case of mistaken identity.

But of course, then how do you explain my recurring dreams?

And the identical reddish-yellow Subarus in the same exact parking lot at the same exact time?

"It's synchronicity, Nana."

"It is," she says.

We are early, and this gives us a chance to study the loading dock and marina across the street and to spec out the ship's check-in procedure for the real SEAmester kids, the ones who are *supposed* to be here.

"We need to stick to our plan to get on board," Nana says.

I want to ask Nana which plan, exactly, she is referring to, since we are pretty much flying by the seat of our pants at this point. Sure, we were able to convince Mom and Dad that my invite onto the *Oceania II* was legit.

You won an essay contest? Sidney, that's fantastic!

Of course you can go.

Which was a good thing, since I had already replied to the message and said, *Dr. Sidney Miller would be honored to attend.*

And yeah, with a little Photoshop doctoring I was able to print out the welcome letter. It wasn't perfect, but my parents were so excited about my academic achievement they didn't look too closely. They didn't see that I spelled *coalition*—as in Global Coalition—wrong.

But what happens after this is anybody's guess.

"We need to observe things for a while. That way we can be prepared for the unexpected," Nana whispers.

"Why are we whispering, Nana?"

She doesn't answer. She holds out her hand, I pass her the binoculars from my backpack, and she presses them to her face.

"What do you see?" I ask.

She answers, "Balloons."

"Balloons?"

"Look for yourself."

It takes me a while to adjust the focus and figure out what I am looking at. The trees in front of us, the metal fence, a bird, a cardboard box, a lone banana, all look so big.

"Holy cow, I can see the brown spots on the peel!"

I take the binoculars away from my eyes, and I realize I'm just seeing the stuff in *this* parking lot. The marina is much farther away. I try again.

Finally, I see water. And boats. I see the pier, the metal planks. Boxes. These big, corrugated storage containers. It all looks very industrial. I move my line of sight slowly right, then left, until I see the check-in area.

"Oh yeah, there! I see the balloons now. Green ones. And oh, look, two long folding tables and signs."

"Signs, what kind of signs?" Nana isn't so much whispering anymore.

"No, not that kind. Just signs, Nana. Poster-board signs."

"What do they say?"

"One says, something clean water . . . Summit something. And the other one says . . . Wait, now I can't see anymore. There's someone in the way. Someone is standing in front of the table."

"Who?" Nana asks.

I turn the toggle on the top of the binoculars to see if that helps, if I can get a closer look.

"It's a kid. A teenager maybe, maybe younger. A boy," I say. "He's talking to someone . . . oh, okay . . . now he's walking toward the SEAmester table. And he doesn't look very happy. He's holding something . . . yeah, I see, he's got his cell phone."

"Perfect," Nana says. She rests her head back. "Trust me. Nothing more distracted and inattentive than an adolescent boy with a phone in his hands."

2.

JEREMY JB "A GUY'S GOTTA PEE" BARNES

I double-check that everything is in order: my QR code app, the clipboard of names, the cardboard box with the package of precut white squares and the pile of tangled see-through plastic badges with the green-and-white lanyards, and the Dramamine bracelets (trust me, you can't forget those). As the SEAmester kids arrive, my job number two, after checking each one in, is to put their name on the square, slip it into the recycled plastic, clip that to the lanyard, and have them put it around their neck before they board.

I can do that.

What I can't do is hold my pee much longer.

The sun bakes hot, and a drip of sweat races down the side of my face by my ear.

Gross.

Across from me, Henry's still setting up. I'm ahead of schedule. No one from the few cars or the shuttle bus seems to be crossing our way yet. I probably have plenty of time to make a quick run.

"Okay if I pee, Henry?" I call to him, and nod toward the building. "I kinda have to pee."

"If a guy's gotta pee, he's gotta pee," Henry says. "Be fast."

"Aye, aye, Captain," I say in my best SpongeBob voice. Since it's probably the hundredth time in ten days I've said that, I don't need to turn back to see Henry rolling his eyes at me.

SIDNEY MILLER

When I'm nervous, I always feel like I have to use the bathroom even when I don't. I *know* I don't because I just used the bathroom at the diner where we had breakfast, and that was less than fifteen minutes ago. It doesn't make sense I'd have to go again.

But you never know.

Besides, I have no idea how long I'll have to be hiding

before I get caught, at which point I will be either thrown in the brig, or made to walk the plank.

"You watch too many movies," Nana says. "But it's always a good idea to use the bathroom before a long trip." She nods once with authority and opens the car door. "Let's go."

We cross the street and head straight through the marina parking lot, which now has quite a few cars, and one white shuttle bus, with bunches of teenagers and their parents spilling out, backpacks shouldered, feet shifting impatiently as their parents administer last-minute instructions, then hug them far too tight given this sweltering heat.

I guess those are the SEAmester kids. I swallow hard at this potentially very bad idea of mine. They look a *lot* older than I do. The boys, not so much, but the girls sure do. They are all way taller than I am.

"There's no way anyone is going to believe I am one of them," I say, kind of to myself, but Nana hears.

"We won't know until we try," she says.

"No, you're right, Nana. How about this?" I say. "I get into the line with the SEAmester kids, at the very end, when things are the most hectic and everything is running late. Like you always say, at some point everything runs late."

I can see the huge, big green boat just off the pier, and

the closer we get, the huger and bigger it looks—angle optics. We are close enough to the check-in table that I can see all the kids and parents starting to line up, and I see the entire banner now.

CLEAN WATER SUMMIT

WELCOME SEAMESTER STUDENTS & GLOBAL SCIENTISTS

Clean water.

And I think: Why is there anything other than *clean* water? It shouldn't even be a phrase, right? It should be redundant. The earth takes care of cleaning the water: evaporation, condensation, precipitation, around and around. Clean water. So maybe Rachel Carson is the reason I am here.

I reach around to feel the canvas bag zip-tied to my backpack, hanging off the side but not dangling. I didn't want Rachel Carson to be bouncing around and get motion sickness.

Can goldfish even *get* seasick?

But now I am wondering if bringing her with me was such a good idea in the first place, or whether any of this idea was a good idea in the first place.

"Nana, I'm just thinking here," I say. "Just because those random, crazy coincidences happened, and there's no way to explain them, doesn't necessarily mean they *mean* something, right?"

She smiles at me in a melancholy sort of way, and I know she's thinking about her husband and the crazy, random chance coincidence that brought them together. He's the reason why I have the name I do, Sidney.

Because I was named after him.

And, of course, my name is the biggest reason why I'm here in the first place.

Still, her face looks so sad. "Nana, I didn't mean it like that. I know everything *means* something, of course it does."

She smiles and takes my hand even though I'm almost thirteen, and even though we are both too hot and gross sweaty to hold hands. We walk a little bit more, a little slower. Then Nana stops and turns to me.

"These signs we see all the time, the universe, these coincidences that we give meaning? They only work if we want them to, Sidney. If you want to turn around and go back home, we can do that."

I shrug. "But Nana, even when you *know* they mean something, how do you know what you're supposed to do?"

"You don't," she says. "And then, all of a sudden, you do."

"Maybe we should go back then?"

Nana gives me a little squeeze, then drops my hand, takes a crumpled napkin from her purse, and wipes her palm. She gives it to me and I do the same.

"Well, either way," she says, leading us into the brick building and pointing me toward a door with a mermaid on it. "You should use the bathroom first. No good decisions are made with a full bladder."

"True. I'll be right back," I tell her.

So I guess I'm not paying attention to where I'm walking, but I still think it's his fault, because as I'm heading in, this kid comes barreling out of the mermen's room so fast he just barely misses banging into me. He doesn't say excuse me or sorry, let alone stop to see if I'm all right, but I see *him*. He's the same boy I saw through my binoculars when Nana and I were sitting in the car.

But what I didn't see then—*angle optics*—I see now.

His T-shirt.

It's blue.

There are letters and numbers printed on the front: 79 AU 196.97.

The chemical symbol for gold.

But if that weren't enough, there's more. The letters and numbers are configured into the shape of a fish, and the fish—made of letters and numbers—is floating inside a round fishbowl.

I don't even bother to use the bathroom. "Nana, Nana, you won't believe this."

She does.

And I know exactly why I'm here.

I know what I am supposed to do.

3.

JEREMY JB "NOT MADE OF WILLPOWER" BARNES

The girl barrels into me as I'm coming out of my bathroom and she's going into the one next to it, the one with the mermaid, nearly knocking me over with her overstuffed backpack, which must weigh more than she does.

I'm about to say something, but she's already changed her mind, turned around, stops and stares at me funny for a second—not me, really, but my T-shirt—then runs to her hippie grandma (or at least some lady with some frizzy white hair) and starts babbling excitedly.

Whatever. It's not like it was my fault.

I head toward the back door and, as I do, try my best to avoid seeing it. The thing I don't want to see, that I missed on my way in. The thing that makes me way more homesick than I realized I am after ten whole days at sea. The *Angry Birds Arcade* video game in the corner.

I even try to block it from my eyes with my hand.

But no luck. I still see it. And weirder than that, like the universe is telling me, "Go on, JB, just one fast game!" there's a small stack of quarters sitting on top.

I mean, I'm not made of willpower, only molecules.

I press the quarters into the slot, and the machine lights up, sending another big wave of homesickness crashing through me because me and Sammi and Sean and Dad all used to play this together, back when we were still one big happy family.

I'm lost in the music and the sounds, and before you know it, three pigs are killed, and only one more game would win me a Jackpot bonus. So, yeah, I put enough quarters in to play just one more, and *Whee! Jackpot! Bonus! Go, me!* But as soon as it's over, I find all my willpower again and rush out the door toward my table. Where a whole bunch of SEAmester kids and their parents are already lined up, looking sweaty and fidgety and mad.

"Sorry, sorry," I call to Henry as I race back to my spot behind the table, "it was a really long leak," which makes all the parents look at me funny. My ears burn red. "Have your

QR codes out and ready," I add, trying to redeem my professionality. "I'll check you in as super-duper fast as I can!"

The good thing about a big line at your table is you don't have time to be nervous about what you're supposed to be doing, so I just dive in, scanning QR codes, slipping name tags in holders on lanyards and snapping Dramamine bracelets on, which is, honestly, a hairy amount of activity for one person. By the time I get to the last kid, the girl with the giant backpack and the hippie grandma, my brain is mush, and my body is sweating real bad.

SIDNEY MILLER

I've got my QR code open on my phone, the barcode that came with my "Dear Dr. Sidney Miller" invite.

We move up. One more SEAmester kid gets signed in, gets smothered in kisses from his parents, and heads to where the little boats will come soon to take us onto the ship. The *Oceania II*.

I'm next.

Like a line of *Tetris* blocks falling into place, I'm still in the game.

"Uh, can you hear me?" The kid in his goldfish T-shirt is holding out his hand so I can give him my phone. "That special code we sent you? You're here for the SEAmester trip, right? You're the last one."

"Uh, yeah. That's right. I'm the last one. I mean, yeah. I'm a real teenager here to go on this research vessel to do research."

Nana gives me a little nudge forward. "Go, Sidney—" She stops herself. She leans in and whispers, which she is not too good at doing, "Is that the name we're using?"

Really, I think we should have worked this out, at least a little bit more. I mean, it's not like this boy didn't just hear what my nana said. But he looks too hot and tired to care. An equally weary green balloon lands slowly on the top of his head, rolls off, then sinks to the ground. He doesn't even feel it.

"Oh, right," I say. "The QR code. Sure, here."

Leaving things to fate, to destiny, to chance and synchronicity, I hand over my phone.

4.

JEREMY JB "EXECUTIVE DECISION-MAKER" BARNES

I scrunch my face with confusion and stare at the girl, my brain kind of melting. Because I'm pretty sure the grandma just called her Sidney. Sidney, like the doctor Sidney Miller, marine biologist from the Monterey Bay Aquarium, I invited.

Huh.

But she's clearly not a doctor marine biologist, *right?*

So there's a SEAmester kid named Sidney, too.

I grab the clipboard, my eyes zooming down the roster of SEAmester kid names, but there's no one by that name, Sidney, first or last.

Of course not.

Panic rises in my throat, and meanwhile, this girl is telling me this whole long weirdo story about her grandma and grandpa, how they were meant to be, and stuff about dreams, and carnivals, and nail polish, and my head starts pounding, because what does all of that have to do with anything?

Still, I'm trying to keep up, because it's clearly important to her—like, I swear, she's almost crying—but I'm also glancing again at my SEAmester check-in list, where there's only one name left not crossed out by me as "arrived." And that's a kid named Alex Mylanakos.

A sour feeling starts pressing on my throat.

"Okay, wait," I say, ignoring what I know I heard her grandma call her and trying to get her to slow down. "So, are you Alex Myla—" I pause, trying to pronounce it properly, then just opt for, "Myla-whatever-this-name-is?" and turn the clipboard to her. "Because this is the only missing SEAmester kid."

"Maybe," she says. "I mean, I could be."

She seems nervous. Her grandma makes a coughing sound.

"It's not multiple choice," I say. "Are you or are you not this Alex Myla-person? Because if you're not, I probably can't let you on."

Her lip quivers. "Probably isn't definitely, though, right?"

"It kind of is."

"But you all invited me, see?" She thrusts her phone at me.

The clincher. There it is.

The message I meant to send to Dr. Sidney Miller and not to her.

"I have a QR code and everything, so technically—"

"I see it," I say. Sweat glides down my T-shirt. I want to run and throw her cell phone in the ocean. But of course, it's not *her* fault.

"So then . . . ?"

I close my eyes.

"Hey, JB, what's taking you?" Henry's voice, calling loud and urgent, startles me. I forgot he was even here. "We're ready to load up the first run!"

I turn toward the dock, where he's heading. So, clearly, he's done with the scientist check-in. Now he's moving the grown-ups from the marina to where the gray inflatables will take them to the ship.

He stops and turns back. "I walkie-talkied your mom and Captain Jim to say we're ready. So *be* ready. Additional RIBs will be back for the rest."

For a second, I'm distracted from my main confusion

about the girl, to this new confusion, because why is he talking about barbecued meat? But then I remember: *rigid inflatable boats!* RIBs. I nod, panic now banging in my chest. I can't even remember RIBs, how am I going to explain this girl who thinks she's coming on our ship?

"I really need this," she says.

Need?

Her grandma nods. "Pretty please," she adds.

"Oh, and JB—" Henry jogs back, waving his clipboard. I hold my own clipboard up, hoping to block the girl from his view. "Oh, and there's a marine biologist, a"—he glances down at his clipboard again—"Dr. Sidney Miller, who confirmed. Said he was coming. Guy is important. World-renowned. Jim put a big red star next to his name. But so far, the dude seems to be a no-show, which is pretty disappointing. If he arrives, no matter what, check him in."

I close my eyes at those words, because now it is all crystal clear. I definitely did this. I invited the wrong Sidney Miller. When I open them again, the dock is kind of spinning, but the girl is still there.

"So, Sidney Miller?" I croak.

She smiles sheepishly.

And I make an executive decision right then and there. Because Captain Jim thinks I'm smart, and isn't that what smart people do?

"So, you're him, then," I say, tapping the name on my SEAmester clipboard. "This kid. Instead. Alex Mylanakos, or whatever. Or *her*, I guess, because Alex can be short for Alexis or Alexandra, right? So, sure, why not? You're her."

She blinks up at me. Confused? Grateful? Scared?

How the heck do I know?

All I know is, for ten days, I've been trying to prove myself, and now this girl isn't leaving and the RIBs are, and I can't let anyone else find out just how stupid I am.

TEN DAYS
EARLIER

5.

JEREMY JB "I AM THE CHICKEN" BARNES

Why did the chicken cross the road?

To get to a plane, that took him to a boat, that took him to a ship, that's floating in the middle of the Pacific Ocean.

Did I say chicken? Because I mean me. *Me*. I am the chicken. And that's where I am: floating in the middle of the stupid Pacific Ocean.

That doesn't sound stupid, you say. *That sounds awesome.* And yeah, I mean, the ocean isn't stupid. The ocean is pretty cool.

I like the ocean plenty from the beach.

On a towel.

With Becky Mars.

But forget Becky Mars, because she broke up with me and stomped on my heart.

So, back to the middle of the ocean. In June. With my mom. When school just got out.

Now, *that* is stupid.

I mean, sure, my supersmart, super-twin, superstar, college-aged siblings Sammi and Sean might like it, but they're way different than me.

Why did the chicken talk to himself?

Because he's on a flipping boat in the middle of the flipping Pacific Ocean with nothing to do, and no other kids his age. Not even close. At least not until we pick up some geek SEAmester kids. Plus, there's been puking. By *me*, that is. Did I mention all the puking going on?

"It's a *ship*, JB, not a boat," Mom keeps correcting me, which is not so respectful of my condition. "A ship can carry a whole boat. A boat cannot carry a ship. And this ship in particular has millions of dollars in advanced engineering, research equipment, and navigational systems. Not to mention new, cutting-edge equipment designed to sweep and vacuum up approximately eighty-eight thousand tons of garbage. If, as we hope, we're successful. I'd think you'd think *that* is awesome."

Yeah, sure. Nothing more awesome than a pile of garbage twice the size of Texas called the Great Pacific Garbage Patch.

To be clear, my mom is the chief scientist of the *Oceania II* and likes all sorts of smart things that other people might not. Other people might prefer football and video games.

"You'll learn stuff about yourself out here, JB," she told me on Zoom exactly three weeks ago today when she broke the news. "Things you might not learn otherwise at home. Plus, you'll unplug and get fresh air. I bet you end up loving it out here."

I looked at Grammie and Pops, who'd been staying at our house to watch me, but they kept their heads down, pretending to eat their dinner. When Mom first said she was going out to sea on the ship, I thought it might be fun to stay with my dad, but then I thought again and realized it was smarter not to even ask.

Why did the chicken have to talk to a judge under oath?

Because even at twelve, when your parents are separating, the judge wants to hear if you want to live with your mom or your dad. And when you say, "Either, I don't know," because none of this is what *you* want, the judge picks your mom, because your dad is a pilot and "travels too much." And soon after that, your mom flies out to the middle of the Pacific Ocean.

I stare at the horizon like Mom told me to do to avoid seasickness, and ignore how the *Oceania II* sways with a sudden gust of wind.

So many things can make a kid have to puke these days.

SIDNEY MILLER

I've learned that if I stay in bed and lie quietly for a minute or two, if I don't start thinking about other things right away, if I keep my eyes closed and I don't look around my room at my Star Wars Lego sets, my desk, my laptop (on my desk), my bobblehead Albert Einstein, my bobblehead Nikola Tesla, and my bobblehead Marie Curie—basically, that is, if I don't fully wake up, if I can just lie here for a minute or two more, I can recall my dream for a little longer. And each time I put more of it down in my journal.

I write:

The sky is huge. There's a lot of blue.

I think I taste salt. When I wake up, there's saltiness.

But maybe I'm crying. I'm not sure. Maybe I am crying in my dream

and also when I wake up.

When you write down your dreams first thing in the morning, you start to remember them more clearly. This is a known fact. It's how brains work. So when I first realized, about two weeks ago, that I was having the same dream over and over, I pulled out an old school notebook, one I had apparently decorated with sparkly shark stickers (no idea why I had them), and tore out the written-on pages from last year's sixth-grade language arts class. And I started recording my dreams.

I write:

Huge boat in the middle of the ocean, rocking.

Am I on it?

Birds. Overhead? On the ground? Loud birds squawking.

White. Sand and birds both white.

I am on the boat, but then I am not. Wet. From the ocean?

Not sure, but over my head.

You have to jot down whatever you remember, even the little fragments, no matter how weird or nonsensical. Because that's how dreams are. Recently, I started another journal—using last year's family arts notebook, which was mostly blank anyway—to record the stuff I was googling, about dreaming and dream analysis.

I wrote:

Dr. Sigmund Freud said dreams are a way of protecting you from things that might be too sad or too scary for you to think about when you are awake, so they come out in weird, confusing stories. Like if you are trying to fly in your dream but you can't really get off the ground, it might mean you feel worried, like a math test coming up or tryouts for the swim team. If you dream about missing your school bus, or not being able to find your locker, or you can't press the buttons on your *phone, maybe you are having insecurity about something. Like trying out for the swim team or an upcoming math test.*

And you'd be surprised to find that dreaming you are in the school cafeteria, then suddenly looking down only to discover you are still in your pajamas, is very common.

"Sidney, did you forget to set your alarm?" My dad knocks three times—scattering the last bits of my dream memory into oblivion—then just opens my door and walks in.

I shut my notebook. "Daaad, I *told* you I am conducting an experiment."

"Well, let's hope a part of that experiment includes getting out of bed. Nana will be here soon."

I love my nana more than anything. She is way cooler than anyone else's grandmother that I know, but I don't need a babysitter. I could easily stay home by myself, all summer if I had to. I know twelve-year-olds who are babysitting other kids already. The problem is my mom thinks I spend too much time by myself already. She doesn't understand that I am perfectly fine by myself. I prefer it, in fact.

Besides, there isn't anyone else I want to spend time with since my best friend, Megan, moved away, and by away, I mean over six thousand miles. To Hong Kong, because her dad got transferred.

Oh wait, wait . . . I remember one more thing. I grab my dream notebook.

I write:

There's someone else there, too.

    In the water?

    On the boat?

    A girl? A boy?

    A girl <u>and</u> a boy?

    Not sure.

6.

JEREMY JB "PART OF THE PROBLEM" BARNES

I'm thinking about a girl and a boy, suddenly, and I don't even know why.

Fine, not any girl and boy, but Becky Mars and me. So, even though Mom said being out to sea will help me like it helped her "get over your father," it apparently isn't doing that yet.

Like Mom and Dad, Becky and me met in middle school, but Mom and Dad stayed together for all of high school, college, and thirteen years after that, with only one break when Dad went into the air force, while Becky and me didn't even make it a whole school year.

So why am I still thinking about the Sparta Spring Dance when we dressed up all spiffy like grown-ups, and how, at the end, Becky finally let me give her a two-second kiss on the lips? Not that I counted *during*, of course. Just estimated *after*.

I glance down at the green-and-white side of the ship, and I realize. *Great work*, Oceania II. *Same exact colors as our school.*

The Sparta Spring Dance was fun—way more fun than a garbage ship. Which is why I'm also thinking about all the hilarious jokes we told at our table with Nicky and his date Miranda, and about how all of us slow danced under the mirror ball, so I don't even hear anyone yelling at me at first—"JB, get down!!!"—until I do and realize I've stepped up onto a narrow metal ledge that lets me hang my top half over the railing's edge.

"Sorry, sorry!" I yell. "Relax, dudette," but I lower my voice on that last part. I drop down standing on tiptoes enough to see Randi with Marco below me in the inflatable boat, heading to the visible edge of the garbage pile.

I watch them motor off, then pull myself up again and watch where the waves stirred by the motor smash up against the base of the hull in refreshing white swooshes, until I get nauseous again.

I close my eyes and count to ten, and when I open them,

the weirdest thing has appeared on the railing in front of me, a silver-blue sparkle shark sticker glinting up at me.

Where'd that come from?

Without thinking, I peel that sucker off and, with one quick flick, send it sailing into the ocean.

My heart sinks.

Dumb!

What else is new?

I just added one more piece of garbage to the ocean.

SIDNEY MILLER

"Yoo-hoo, Jamie. It's me!" My mom is shouting at another mom on the whole other side of the fairgrounds. She is waving so much, like those people with yellow reflector vests and orange batons who guide the planes onto the runway. That's how badly she wants me to make new friends, and I don't know who to feel sorry for, her or me.

No, me.

Definitely me.

Because what I really want is for my best friend to not have moved away.

"Over here," my mom calls out again. This time the woman seems to have heard, and she waves back.

I wasn't really keen on coming here to the fair, but yesterday my mom said I needed to be around people my own age.

Nana said, "What am I, chopped liver?"

Which I thought was pretty hilarious, but the humor didn't have any effect on my parents' mutual decision for me to come to the fair, because I am now standing face-to-face with a girl from my class, Rebecca Jamison. If my mom knew that just last week Rebecca told her own cousin she was too fat to sit with her in the cafeteria, she'd never be doing this. But then again, you never know how desperate a mother can get when she thinks her daughter has no friends.

"You know my daughter, Sidney, don't you?" my mom says.

"Yes, of course," Mrs. Jamison says. "Who could forget such a pretty girl with such an unusual name."

Rebecca rolls her eyes. No one sees. Well, I do.

Since I am not that pretty, and Sidney is not uncommon at all, this is what is known as a platitude.

"You girls were in the same kindergarten, weren't you?" Mrs. Jamison goes on.

"I'm not sure," Rebecca says.

Rebecca knows, absolutely, that we were in the same kindergarten class and the same third *and* fifth grade—Mrs. Daugnaut, Mr. Chopsky, and Ms. Keiley, respectively. We weren't friends then, and since the most likely predictor of future events is past events, we probably aren't going to be friends now.

"Oh yeah, now I remember," Rebecca says, suddenly cheerful, but I can tell by the way she's smiling that she's got something else on her mind altogether. "Hey, Sidney, wanna go on the Dragon Coaster with me?"

I knew it! Something is up.

My mother, of course, is thrilled by the suggestion, so there is no time to explain the potentially nefarious nature of Rebecca's offer. Besides, grown-ups don't always need to know the whole truth. It can be hard for them to handle, especially my mom.

Here's why:

My parents are divided into two anxiety factions. My dad worries about physical things, like me getting injured, falling off my bike, a bad reaction to the flu shot, cutting myself while slicing a bagel, choking on the hard candy they give away at the diner cashier counter. Things like that.

My mom worries about everything else. The emotional stuff. Which is why we are here at the fair.

"That's a great idea, Rebecca," my mom answers for me. "Sidney loves roller coasters."

The sun is only now beginning to lower behind the cut-out skyline of what I think is supposed to be the ancient city of Baghdad. The lights on the rides have been on all day, but now they're starting to twinkle, and drops of wet forming on the grass are sparkling. It is simple dew-point condensation and light refraction, but it makes everything look magical.

Who doesn't like a good roller-coaster ride?

So I say:

"Sure."

My mom chirps, "Okay then, sounds great. Which way to the Dragon Coaster?" But Rebecca doesn't move, so no one else does either.

"Well . . . ," Rebecca starts out slowly. "We were thinking we could go by ourselves."

We were?

Both moms straighten their backs like a gust of wind just hit them in the face, a gust of wind with a terrible smell; their faces squinch up.

I guess Rebecca's mom is a worrywart, too.

There are plenty of kids from middle school who have been coming to the town fair by themselves since fifth grade, some even dragging younger siblings along with them. The whole fair is set up in the back of the elementary school, surrounded by the Little League field on one side, the fire station and library parking lot on the other. So as far as fairs go, it's really small and as safe as you can get.

"Sure, we'll be sure to stay back." My mom laughs. "You two go ahead. You won't even know we're here."

Mrs. Jamison is nodding emphatically.

"C'mon, Mom," Rebecca whines. "I mean *really* by ourselves. We both have phones. We'll be fine."

Then she goes for the jugular vein of mothers everywhere.

"You don't want the other kids to think we're losers, do you?" Rebecca says so sweetly you'd think there is syrup sliding down her throat. "No one in our grade comes here with their parents."

Now she looks at me. "Right, Sidney?"

Before I can explain that there isn't a single kid in our

whole school who would ever call Rebecca Jamison a loser, my mother blurts out, "Well, it's okay with me if it's okay with you, Jamie." Can you believe that's her name?

Mrs. Jamison drops open her mouth, inhales deeply, then shuts it again, then opens it. "Sure you have your phone?"

Rebecca reaches into the back pocket of her jeans and displays her bedazzled cell phone. "Fully charged," she says. "We'll meet you back at the fire station in two hours."

"One hour." Apparently my mother has, at least, partially come back to her senses.

"An hour and a half?" Rebecca tries.

Jamie Jamison takes her cell phone and looks at the time. "Hour and fifteen. That makes our rendezvous at exactly seven forty-six. Not one minute later. Got it?"

"Got it," Rebecca agrees, and in a final shocker, she takes my hand, leaving me no choice. As soon as we are out of sight of the moms, she lets go.

"Here's the deal," she stops and tells me. "You stay out of my way, I'll stay out of yours. We meet at the fire station ten minutes before we're supposed to. We both enter from the baseball-field side just in case they are there early and see us coming. From the baseball field, got it?"

"Little League," I say. "Not baseball."

"What?" She is annoyed that I am eating into her one hour and fifteen minutes, I suppose.

I can hear the tinny music from the Ferris wheel, a loud burst of laughter from somewhere, and squeals from the petting zoo.

"It's a Little League field. A baseball field would be bigger, the distance between the bases would be thirty feet longer."

"You're weird." Rebecca is adjusting her outfit, rolling up the bottoms of her shorts and tying her sweatshirt around her waist, even though it's probably only sixty-five degrees out. "Just be here at . . . at . . . whatever. At ten minutes before seven forty-six."

"Seven *thirty*-six. That was a hard one."

"Whatever."

And then I'm alone.

I really, really miss Megan. I'm never going to make another friend again, and it's going to be a really, really long summer without her.

7.

JEREMY JB "MISSING TIME" BARNES

7:36 p.m.

How did *that* happen?

Clearly time goes missing when you're out to sea staring at water and drifting bits that eventually clog up into one big pile of floating garbage.

Well, kind of a pile. But not exactly.

Some scientists call it a patch, some a pile, but neither of those are really correct. It's not like you can see garbage heaped up or anything, and it's not like some small little patch. It's more like someone dumped a giant-sized can of vegetable soup into the ocean everywhere, and it clogged here in this spot, and the peas and carrots aren't vegetables, but junk made of plastic and rubber and stuff. If that's not bad enough, this isn't the only clogged spot. There are lots of them. At least five. Mom calls it an island because I guess it sounds prettier like that.

The way the garbage all gets to these spots, Mom explained, is by these things called gyres, which are systems of wind and friction and currents that work together to blow all the garbage into one place. And the Great Pacific Garbage Patch is the biggest. But that doesn't mean there isn't more garbage everywhere. Pretty much where there is ocean, there is garbage, I kid you not.

The majority of this *island* is made up of the smallest junk your eyes can barely see: millions, or billions, of colorful microplastics and microbeads, those little things companies put in shampoo or body wash or slime.

And all this time, you think, well, if they're in shampoo, they must dissolve and wash away, but they don't. They disappear down the drain or get dumped into kitchen trash cans, then wind up in rivers and inlets, then drift and float with the wind out to sea. Same with the plastic bags, and soda rings, and toothbrushes, and rubber gloves, and water bottles, and straws, and face masks, and plastic cups, and even bigger stuff—no kidding—things like tires and other auto parts, and computers, and cell phone cases, even a couch and its matching floating cushions are in this one clogged pile.

And now a sparkle shark sticker that dumb old me contributed.

Which is why my mother and her team have been studying the island, plus trying to install a giant water vacuum system that everyone was super hopeful about at first, but now they're not so sure because it may or may not help much to clean pieces of it up.

And why I'm here with them, the only human under the age of twenty-five.

The only half-good news is that next week, a bunch of kids called Summer SEAmester students will arrive from high schools around the country because they won some essay contest about why they want to be a marine biologist or cleaner-upper of floating garbage or something smart like that. They'll spend one week on board and get special credit, which will look awesome on their college applications.

"You'll be able to spend time with them *and* learn with them," Mom told me, like I'm not a C– middle schooler and, so, like the last person on earth any overachieving

SEAmester high school kid will want to spend their time with. "We may even be able to get you extra credit."

Whatever. So, my C– will go to a nice solid C.

Which reminds me, Mom also said something this morning about a job for me starting tomorrow, because by then, my seasickness should be over. Also, she said, "Captain Jim and I have a few different ways in mind that you can help us. Computer and internet stuff. Stuff that is perfect for your skill set."

So, first: Who knew I had a skill set?

And, second, yeah, in case you've never been on a research ship, there is definitely the internet out here.

In fact, even if I don't really want to be out here, I have to admit, the ship is pretty cool. Not fancy like a cruise ship—not that I've ever been on one of those—but it does have a wet lab and dry lab, a kitchen (the "galley"), "the mess," which is a dining hall where you all eat, a gym, a big, noisy, industrial laundry room, and a room called the lounge, with coffee makers and a big-screen TV where I've seen some of the team playing *Mario Kart* late at night.

The only thing different is that pretty much everything big and heavy on the ship, like tables and chairs, are bolted down, so they don't go flying and impale you through the head in a storm. It also has a corridor full of small sleeping cabins, most with bunk beds, plus the captain's cabin, which is the biggest, and where Captain Jim gets to sleep. Some of the crew share cabins, and others have them all to themselves, which Mom says will change when the scientists and SEAmester kids all come on board.

"There will have to be some doubling and tripling up then."

I share a cabin with my mom now, which sounds weird, but the truth is, she's barely in it, and when she does come in, she's so crazy tired, she falls sound asleep and is gone before I even wake up again.

A few other places to know are the bridge, where you drive the ship, the hospital, which is more like a small nurse's office in an elementary school, and the meeting room, where the crew shares their daily progress. In two and a half days on board, mostly puking, I've only seen some of the rooms, and it's all kind of fuzzy, like the time that goes missing out here and everything else that feels way stranger on sea than on land.

Like how, now, 7:36 is already 7:52 and so the sky is turning to dusk, even though I haven't done *anything* except stand here endlessly watching over the railing to see if I can maybe spot dolphin or shark fins, or at least the white-gray shadows of marlins or belugas or sperm whales skimming underneath, or catch the see-through purple shimmer of a Portuguese man-of-war bobbing on the surface like some ruffly soup dumpling except with long, deadly tentacles trailing just below the waves. Because those are all down there somewhere. Marco and Randi and Vance and Sabira and Henry have all recorded seeing them, plus taken photos and posted them to the ship's Instapik page (Oceania II if anyone out there wants to follow).

Instapik photos or not, I spy nothing but endless water and waves, and watching those makes my stomach slosh, so I decide to break Mom's number one rule and pull out my cell phone because I'm missing my friends so bad right now, especially Nicky, and other people, too, like my dad, and honestly, this kind of homesickness feels almost as bad as puking.

But just as I'm about to press Nicky's number, my brain snaps to it and hears Mom yelling for me. "Here you are, JB! We've all been looking for you. Dinner's ready in the mess. Where were you?" Like there are a million places other than right here on deck I might be.

Still, I'm relieved to get going, and more relieved about something else, too, because just as I turn to go in, my eye catches a small little something glinting in the sunset, and it's the stupid shark sticker, the same exact one I littered with, that has somehow miraculously found its way stuck back to the railing like a sparkly stroke of luck, and so I walk over and peel off that sucker, and put it, not in the ocean, but in my pocket.

SIDNEY MILLER

Even Nana has never let me eat a hot dog. I mean, an old-fashioned all-beef nitrate-filled hot dog. I've had the fake organic chicken ones plenty of times. I'm sure Rebecca is off doing something way worse with her mom-free time, but me? I am going to have a hot dog.

"You want kraut with that?"

"Yes, please. Thank you. Is there mustard?"

"On the counter." The woman inside the truck hands me my dog and points.

It certainly tastes better going down than it does when

I'm done. But I suppress an encroaching stomachache in order to try another parental-off-limits fairground treat, a candied apple. Bad choice. The outside is hard, falls apart in chunks, sticks to my back teeth, dribbles red into my hand, and doesn't even taste good. The apple inside is mushy and mealy.

The apple-to-flimsy-Popsicle-stick ratio is way off.

I need to throw this thing away quickly.

It's pretty hard to find a trash can, so no wonder there's so much litter everywhere on the ground: a plastic fork, no, two plastic forks, someone's pink ten-ride bracelet, a light blue disposable face mask, a purple lighter, and one of those mini basketballs flattened into a pancake. When I finally find the garbage bins, the recycling one marked CANS AND BOTTLES ONLY has a few balled-up candy wrappers and a half-finished—chocolate?—milkshake at the bottom. The other bin, marked TRASH, is overflowing with paper bags and water bottles sticking out like octopus arms, and now a candied apple that I manage to stuff in.

I notice I've wandered pretty far from the main fairgrounds. The merry-go-round music, the voices, talking and laughing, the clanking of the Ferris wheel, and the squeals and screams from the giant slide, are all behind me. Everything has a bluish tinge as the sun goes down, and the long shadows are disappearing into dusk. It's almost as if, here by the arcade, away from the rides, it's a whole different fair.

My sneakers are squishy from the wet grass, soaked all the way through to my socks, but it's quieter here. A good place to wait out the next thirty-six minutes of my freedom.

"Wanna win a goldfish, young lady?"

"No thanks," I say without looking to see who is talking to me.

But then I do. I turn and look, and even though I've never seen this place, or this man, or this carnival booth before, it's so strangely familiar. And then I remember.

My dream.

"All's you need to do is toss the life preserver onto the main topsail. Three tries. One dollar." The man stands in the worn-down grass, just in front of his booth, and his booth is a boat painted green on the bottom, white on the top half. The boat from my dream.

"If one toss lands on the ship's deck you get three more rings . . . for half price. Just two quarters," he calls out to me.

Okay, so this boat is made of plywood, with holes cut

out for portals and a real fake-plastic anchor hanging over the side. But it's a boat, just like in my recurring dream.

"Hey, kiddo. You wanna play or not?"

Behind the plywood boat is a table set up with bowling pins. On a shelf behind the bowling pins is a fishbowl, and inside the fishbowl is a goldfish.

I've never had a pet before because without the slightest bit of empirical evidence, my mom worries that I am allergic to pet dander. I am certain that fish don't shed, but more than that, this goldfish looks lonely. And so am I.

I decide on a sidearm toss. Just as I predicted, the ring wobbles in the air like a poorly thrown Frisbee and drops into the dirt.

"Two more chances, kid."

The pins are so close together there's no way it's going to land flat onto the neck of one of those pins. Calculating, I should aim for the pin farthest to the outside corner and toss it at an angle.

"Can I throw my last two at the same time?" I ask the man.

"Sure, why not?" he says. "But it counts as two. You don't get another one unless you pay for it."

"Fine."

I have no idea what makes me think I have a chance at

this at all. But, déjà vu, I feel like I've been here before. I lay one ring directly over the other, to give it a little more weight and balance, and I aim for that outermost bowling pin.

Just before I let go, I feel a swoosh of cool air like wind coming from somewhere that's not here, and the two rings spin flatly through the air, dropping perfectly on target.

"What's that?" Rebecca asks me.

"*Who* is that, would be the correct question." I hold my water-filled plastic bag by its twist-tied top protectively in my fist, a tiny goldfish swimming around inside.

"It's Rachel," I say.

"Rachel? You named a goldfish Rachel?"

We are both early. The moms aren't here yet.

"Well," I start to explain. "Rachel *Carson*. You know, the marine biologist."

The look on Rebecca's face tells me that not only does she have no idea what I am talking about, she has no interest, either.

Mrs. Jamie Jamison calls out from about ten yards away. "Girls, girls, there you are! Right on time."

They hurry over to us. I see that my mom is trying hard not to look overly relieved, and a big wave of love washes over me. She's a really great mom who just happens to worry a lot.

Tree peepers are singing by the edge of the woods. It's 7:52 when we say our goodbyes, and we both head off in opposite directions. Rebecca turns back around and calls out, fakely.

"See you later, Sidney."

My mom puts her arm around my shoulder as we walk to our car. I know how disappointed she'll be when she hears that Rebecca Jamison and I didn't actually hold hands and ride the Dragon Coaster together. But that can wait.

She is rummaging around in her purse for her keys. "Well, looks like you've made a new friend," my mom says.

I'm still hiding Rachel Carson behind my back.

"Actually, I have," I say.

8.

JEREMY JB "KING OF THE INTERNETS" BARNES

"So, we could use your help finding some folks, JB," Captain Jim says, the minute I sit down at the mess-room table. He's pointing at me with a mini pig-in-the-blanket hot dog, which he promptly pops into his mouth. "I hear you're quite an expert navigating the web, and we need to locate and invite a bunch of pretty well-known scientists, oceanographers, and marine biologists to join us," he adds, not yet finished chewing.

"Yeah, maybe he can invite Rachel Carson," Marco laughs.

"Who?" I ask, stuffing a bite of Chicki's amazing breadcrumb mac 'n' cheese into my mouth, having only just realized how hungry I am. Chicki is the ship's chef and pretty much everything she makes is delicious. At least when you're not too seasick to eat it.

"Never mind, sweetie. He's teasing you," Mom says.

Okay, fine. Whatever.

"Anyway, JB, they may be a bunch of wise guys, but they sure aren't very well versed in social media, so we could really use your expertise in finding some people."

"Hey, speak for yourself," Vance says. "We're Oceania II on Twitter *and* Instapik. That's all me! I set those up. You should check them out. And follow us. And retweet. Make it happen."

Sabira rolls her eyes, but I like Vance. He's friendly, not bossy like Randi and Marco can be, and always wears a baseball cap and funny T-shirts that say things that have to do with the mission, but kind of sarcastic. Like, yesterday's shirt said GIGO, which he told me means, "Garbage In, Garbage Out," and the day before that was one with the famous *Jaws* movie poster with the shark coming up out of the water, only the shark is made of red plastic drinking straws and it says STRAWS instead of JAWS underneath. Today he's wearing a black T-shirt with a mustard-yellow fish in a bowl. Across the top it reads 79 AU 196.97, which, actually, I have no idea what that means.

Mom must catch me looking at it, because she leans in and whispers, "Atomic number for gold, get it?" And clearly I don't fast enough, so she adds, "Think periodic table of elements, from the Latin *aurum* for gold. So, a goldfish, see?"

I nod, then blurt like I knew it myself, "Nice goldfish, Vance," and Mom quick says, "Well, we all have those, so if you want one, I have extras. I'll give you one of mine."

Great. Just what I always wanted.

"Okay, back to the task at hand, please, hon," Captain Jim says to Mom, causing everyone to look up fast at the same time. Mom shoots him a bug-eyed glance, probably because it's not a very feminist thing to call a world-class scientist like my mother. "Hon . . . I mean, *hon*-estly," he corrects himself. "As in, honestly, Bronwyn, don't we have the perfect special project earmarked for JB?"

Sabira coughs, and Marco laughs a snorty laugh, and now Mom shoots them both the same bug-eyed glance, so I'm really confused about what's going on.

"Captain Jim is right," Mom says, bringing us back to the subject, which I remember now is me being an expert at social media stuff. Which actually could be good, because, enough of this sea stuff, I could use a few hours on the internet. Check out Nicky's Instapik. Share a few cool photos of my own. "We think you can handle it," she adds.

"Yes," Captain Jim jumps back in. "Bet you prove genius, impressing us all. But we need you right on it. You can use my computer in my cabin. It's roomier and the Wi-Fi is better. I'm out by 0600, so you can get on it first thing tomorrow." He winks at Mom and she smiles, calmer, but something about the whole exchange makes my guts squirm.

I push Chicki's mac 'n' cheese away and squint at him.

Captain Jim is not at all a captain like you'd think, like Captain Sully, or even Cap'n Crunch, in a neat black hat and crisp white uniform. Or especially Dad, who always looks sharp and professional when he's at work in his navy blue uniform with the shoulder stripes, which all mean something, and his cap with the gold bars and braid.

Captain Jim is the opposite. Most of the time, he doesn't wear a uniform. He wears jeans with Muck boots and old concert T-shirts. And his face, which is older than Dad's, has eyes that crinkle when he smiles. Oh, and his long gray hair is tied back in a ponytail.

A *ponytail.*

"So what do you say?" Mom asks. "Think you could locate these scientists for us and make initial contact?"

"Yeah, sure. I guess."

"Well, don't sound so enthusiastic," she says.

"Of course he is, right, JB?" Captain Jim says. He leans forward and chucks me on the shoulder. I'm not sure I'm good with that.

"Yeah, totally," I say.

"Just to be clear, you're simply locating people and sending a letter via email. Someone from the team has already drafted the letters. Individualized them. I'll have them forwarded to you in the morning, to your mom's email, if you don't use one. Your job is to find as many of these people as you are able, and get the invites out to them. If you can't locate a direct email or web page, maybe they have a social media account, or whatever. That's why we need you. You know all this better than we do."

"How many in all?" I ask.

"Not more than—" Captain Jim stops, looking to Mom for confirmation. She nods and starts bobbing her head like she's thinking and counting.

"Maybe twenty or so?" Mom says. "But if we can get even five or six to commit . . ."

"Give or take a few," Captain Jim continues, plowing forward. "Some of the most renowned marine experts from all over the world. This whole thing is a bit of a Hail Mary—er, a long shot—but it's pretty exciting, too. What we've decided to do here is create an impromptu global summit."

"For publicity," Sabira adds softly.

"*And* for the good of the order," Henry adds.

"Of course, it may be more impromptu than doable at this point," Randi chimes in, with her typical sarcasm.

"But we really have no choice," Sabira says. "We need to try something."

No clue what any of them are talking about anymore, so I just keep nodding.

"What you really need to know, JB, is that this is all short notice, so we need you to take it seriously. This will be a big opportunity for us to do something newsworthy and garner some needed publicity for the mission. Without it, well . . ." Mom stops and looks down. "Without it, we fear the end of our grant money, hence the end of the mission. So we're really hoping this works and that these scientists might find it in their hearts and their schedules to be spontaneous."

"Spontaneity. The first hallmark of scientists," Marco says, and Randi laughs.

They talk more about that, whatever Marco said, but by now, I'm totally lost, and just want to be clear on my actual job. Because Captain Jim thinks I'm an expert, so I don't want to screw it up.

"So you give me a list of names," I clarify, "and I just need to find them, right?"

"Exactly," Captain Jim says. "Find as many as possible, send the corresponding individualized letter we give you. A cut-and-paste job, so long as you get the right letter to the right person. We're sure you can handle that."

"Yeah, absolutely," I say. "And you need it by when?"

"Yesterday," Randi says, and this time Mom manages a laugh.

"It is kind of true," Captain Jim says. "But no pressure. You've got this. How about end of tomorrow?"

SIDNEY MILLER

As soon as I got home from the fair last night, I put Rachel Carson in a glass mixing bowl that I snuck out of the kitchen. I realized I didn't have any food for her, but Google told me goldfish can go for three days without eating. Yeah, well, so can humans, but we'd be really hungry. Another search told me goldfish can eat frozen peas as long as you take the tough outer peel off.

But this morning, I really need to figure out something more permanent, and definitely more homey, for Rachel Carson. Maybe some colorful gravel, a few plants? And a toy deep-sea diver? For sure, a real fish tank.

I also need to tell my mom, which I do.

"It's a lot of responsibility, taking care of another living being," she says.

"Isn't that what you want? For me to learn responsibility?" I'm not sure she's ever said that exactly, but it sounds right.

I've already gotten up and made my bed. My clothes from last night are in my hamper. I even thoughtfully picked up all the Legos from the floor, because nothing hurts quite as much as stepping on one in bare feet. But while my mom is talking, she's straightening up my room.

"Well, of course I do, sweetie," she says. "But I don't think that mixing bowl is right for it."

"I know. And not 'it,'" I correct my mother. "Her."

"Her?"

I nod. "Rachel Carson."

"You named your goldfish Rachel Carson? Like the famous naturalist?"

"Marine biologist," I correct my mother again. "Yeah, her."

She lifts my bobbleheads one at a time and wipes the shelf with the sleeve of her bathrobe. "And you'll have to teach me how to take care of it—*her*—when you're at summer camp."

"It's easy . . . Wait, what? I'm not going to camp this summer." It never even entered my brain that such a thing was being considered, let alone decided. "Not without Megan."

We both hated summer camp. But at least last year, we had each other. Maybe it would have been better if last summer hadn't been record-breaking hot, with record-breaking heat waves. Or if the camp had air-conditioning, which it didn't.

Most of the time, Megan and I tried to sneak away from all the activities that made you sweat, which was every one: capture the flag, kickball, hiking, nature scavenger hunts. When the sun went down, the air cooled off, but the bugs came out, so even flashlight tag was miserable. The very first night, three kids had to go to the nurse's office for Benadryl and calamine lotion.

The one relief from the heat and the bugs was the water, and that was a whole other kind of awful. Swim lessons were run by Elsa the Evil One. If she wasn't blowing her whistle telling us to kick, kick, kick, she was twirling the whistle string around her finger, one way and then the other, like a whip.

After dinner there was a mandatory sing-along that usually involved standing up and doing hand motions in unison.

No, there was no way I was going back there.

Not without Megan.

My mother pulls out the chair at my desk and sits down. She crosses her legs and inhales a deep breath, always a signal that she has just been thinking of something serious and she is about to say it. Sometimes she touches her fingers to her forehead and then expands her hand as if she is releasing her thoughts from her brain into the air.

"Well, look," she begins. "I understand all that, and we

are not going to force you to go to camp. At the same time, we're not going to let you stay home all summer and watch TV."

I open my mouth to object.

"Wait," my mother says. "I'm not done."

I close my mouth.

"But maybe we can come up with something in between."

"A compromise?"

"A negotiation."

When my mother stands and steps on a stray Lego piece from the *Millennium Falcon* that I must have missed, she lets out a howl that brings my father and my nana rushing into my room, which turns out to be fortuitous. Not for my mother, obviously, but this way, we hash out my summer plan with all parties present and in agreement.

9.

JEREMY JB "PLEASE, NO MORE PUKING" BARNES

I wake up in the middle of the night, which turns out to actually be dark morning, because, whoa, it's stormy outside. The ship is rocking, and there's zero light coming in through the porthole. On the dresser thingy in front of me, Mom's Jacques Cousteau bobblehead with his red beanie cap is bobbling all around.

"Good morning to you, not!" I say to Mr. Cousteau, before he pitches forward and slides off the desk and onto the floor.

A guy could get hurt around here.

I crawl onto my knees and look out the porthole, but everything is gray waves, like literally ocean water sloshing at my eyes through the glass. Which is when I realize, yeah, I'm totally queasy again.

Here I go, back to puking all day.

But no time for that, because I also realize, it's actually 0800 hours (ship time), and I have work to do. Lots of it if I'm not going to let the crew down.

I get out of bed, setting my legs wide for balance, plus holding my arms out like I'm surfing as another big wave sways the ship up and down, up and down. *Puke.* Yet, even in this weather, Mom's bed is empty.

I pull on my new 79 AU 196.97 "goldfish" T-shirt (hey, I don't have a huge supply of clothes I brought along), jeans, and sneakers, and search through the small dresser drawer for the acupressure seasick bands Mom put on me the first day. I'd finally taken them off last night, thinking I was done with them. I wrap one around each wrist, making sure the little metal button presses where my pulse is, then brush my teeth, wash my face, and sweep some tap water through my hair to try to keep the popper pieces from popping up.

As I head out of the cabin, I see a note slipped under the door, my name on top: *JB*, in handwriting that's not Mom's. And under that,

The hunt is on! Here are the names and some minimal information.
    Stop up on the bridge to get my key.

The letters that get copied and pasted
are in a Google doc, link in your mom's
email. She texted you her log-in. Be sure
to send each note to the correct person!
Thanks for your help and expertise!
　　We're counting on you.
　　Jim

I stare at that last part for more than a few seconds, especially that word *expertise*, and wait for the next big wave of
nausea to pass.

Expertise.

I don't think that word has ever been used to describe
me before. Sean and Sammi, who are both molecular and
biological sciences majors at the University of Colorado,
maybe. But me? Hopeful starting quarterback for the Sparta
Knights? Never. And now, here's Captain Jim, trusting me to
be smart and do good work. And for starters, I can barely
read the names.

　　Zhang Liu, PhD—Hong Kong
　　Ian Agus—oceanographer, Australia
　　Samara Redmond—UK, Intl Marine Litter?
　　Nicholas Gardner Johns—ask Marco

Bana or Banya Sinan, PhD—Syria…
TX, now, maybe?

Dr. Sidney Miller—marine biodiversity
podcast. Mont Bay Aq.? "Mind of an
Octopus," <u>Science Today</u>…

Zhang Longping—U China, Dept of
Oceanography

Saoirse McDonnell—US/Wisconsin

Robert Dannon—U Mass
oceanography/marine sci dept

Benjamin S. Samuels—?

Thomas (Tom) Petrovsky

? Aliku Bekele (don't know if spelling is
right)—oceanographer/filmmaker

? Loreen Frain (not sure if she's still
teaching…)

Stephen Burgenhill (Boston University)

Alice Reade (Augusta, ME—adjunct at
U?)

Hans Voss—Vienna, Austria (ask Sabira
for more info)

J. Flanzenberg—NY, NY, doc filmmaker/
adjunct Stony Brook

Coe Hughes—ichthyologist, Seattle
If you finish these, we can think of more.

Panic floods my chest.

There are question marks everywhere, like they're not even sure how to spell all of them or what their jobs are. So how the heck will I find them all?

I shove the list in my back pocket and head down the narrow corridor, past the other cabins, periodically having to hold on to things as the ship weathers another wave. As I press forward, I try to distract myself, letting my eyes scan the busy walls with their levers and power plates and hoses and life jackets and hatchets and other safety equipment everywhere. Past here is the dry lab, where I can already see Sabira, Randi, and Henry working, heads down, at their stations.

When I reach the stairs to the bridge, I stop in my tracks. Something occurs to me. Even though the storm is still going and the ship is still rocking a bit, the wave of nausea has passed. Maybe I'm actually adjusting, becoming a pro at all this. I pull the piece of paper out from my pocket, this time with new confidence, *expertise* coursing through my veins.

We have a plan and this is what it is: I can stay home for the summer with Nana non-babysitting sitting me, as long as once a day we do something educational. So after my mom and dad leave for work, Nana and I put our minds to it. She says Chikki's Salon is the best place to put on our thinking caps.

A little bell over our heads jangles when we walk in the door of the nail spa, and a pretty lady who looks very busy behind the counter, without looking up, asks us what we want.

"Manicure, pedicure," my nana answers. "For me and my granddaughter."

The woman smiles politely. "Toes first," she says, and she tells us to pick our colors. Then she hurries off to get our pedicure chairs ready while we stand in front of a wall of tiny bottles, arranged in hues from dark red to deep purple, Ballet Slippers to Tequila Sunrise to You're in the Navy Now.

My nana goes right for the electric reds, picking up a bottle. "'Never on a Sunday.' Now, what do you think that's supposed to mean?" She laughs that wonderful laugh she has, turns to me, then stops laughing. "Never mind. So now, how is our Miss Rachel Carson?"

I pick up a pink bottle that reads Sinful. I put it back down. "She's good. Dad got me a real fishbowl to put her in." I tell my nana, "So now she's got a little home."

"That's nice. Everyone needs a home," my nana says. "I'm going to try this one, Girls' Night Out."

Nana takes the bottle of red nail polish and heads over to the row of reclining chairs where our two warm, scented footbaths are waiting. "Take your time, my shayna maydel."

That's what she calls me, because that's what *her* nana called her. "Pretty girl" in Yiddish.

Purple, maybe?

I can't decide.

Last time we came here, I picked yellow and had to spend two weeks looking like a corpse until it finally chipped enough and I could pick it off completely. Green, maybe? No, too weird. Red, like my nana's? Too old ladyish.

Honestly, I really don't care that much. My favorite thing at the nail salon is the electric chair massage.

So I grab the first blue bottle I see and I hurry over to join my nana.

Once we are all settled, our feet soaking and our heads resting back, my nana asks me, "So what educational thing do you think we should do today?"

"Maybe a project, Nana."

"Good idea."

Like I said, I love my nana more than anything in the world, but I try not to look at her feet. I bet when she was young she had really pretty toes, but not so much anymore.

"So like what?" I ask.

I look around at the other ladies getting their nails done. Most everyone is by themselves, sitting quietly looking down at their phones, poking them and scrolling through with one long fingernail. One teenager sort of girl is wearing earbuds. I wonder what music she's listening to, but she's not bobbing her head or tapping her feet, so maybe it's a podcast.

"Hey, Nana, how about a podcast?"

"Great idea," she asks. "So what would you talk about?"

"I don't know."

"Something you're really interested in. Something you care about."

"Dreams," I say. The only thing I can think of.

"I dream about your grandpa all the time." I see tears forming in my nana's eyes just remembering him. My grandpa died the year before I was born, which is why they named me Sidney. It was his name.

"Did I ever tell you about how your grandpa and I met?" she asks me.

Of course she has. She tells the story a lot, but I want to hear it again, and I know it makes her feel better to talk about him.

"Tell me, Nana."

And she does, how once upon a time, there was a young woman who liked to walk in the woods by her house, nearly every day. Every now and then she would pass another person, but mostly the woods were empty, and she liked it that way. Then one day, the young woman saw a man. He was walking alone, too. Quietly.

"And he was really cute, right, Nana?"

"He was beautiful."

"So they started meeting up and walking together, right?"

"We started meeting up, and it was the best part of my day."

But the most amazing thing about the story was that the man had also been walking in the woods for many years and he had been lonely, too, but they had never seen each other. Not once. Until they did. And they fell in love.

"Like magic," I said.

The woman who is doing my pedicure looks up. "It's called synchronicity," she says. "It is the moment in time when suddenly we become aware of a deeper connection to the universe. We realize that something that seems random has more meaning than our individual self."

"Is that what it's called?" my nana asks. "Synchronicity."

"It can happen to anyone, anywhere, at any time." The woman holds up a bottle of nail polish and asks me, "Is this the color you want?"

But I'm still in the woods seeing my nana and my grandpa, so I don't even look. "Yeah, thank you," I say.

The woman shakes the bottle and gives it one hard smack on the bottom with the palm of her hand. She reads the label aloud. "Pretty color," she says. "'Oceania.'"

10.

JEREMY JB "I CAN'T UNSEE THAT NOW" BARNES

Key to Captain Jim's cabin obtained, I let myself in and sit at his cushy desk and start searching names, but almost immediately, my screen goes crazy with a zooming cartoon bee wearing glasses. "BuzzNet Podcasts, Bzzzznet!" the bee says, the words flashing so much I have to reboot the computer to get him to go away. Once that's done, I reread the instruction email he forwarded to me.

Hey, JB,

Attached are 18 individualized letters, one for each person on the list. Once you find their contact info, simply:

1. Find their corresponding invite with their name on top.

2. Copy, paste, send!

Any trouble, please reach out to Marco, Randi, or Sabira.

Thanks again,

Cap. Jim

Easy peasy. Right?

I google Zhang Liu in the location listed next to his name—Hong Kong. He comes up fast in all sorts of articles, or at least an L. Zhang does, and that takes me to the Chinese university, Chinese University, where he teaches. There, I get to use more of my expertise skills, because there are lots of departments, and it takes me a few more minutes to find his. I click on that link and it takes me to department contacts, then to the actual web page and the friendly-looking face of a dude standing in a lab coat, in front of a tank with an octopus in it.

A live freaking octopus, so that's pretty cool.

There's a video you can play, but it's all in Chinese, so I can't really learn much from that.

I ex out and scroll down, and find his office hours and email.

Find the person. Check.

Find the note with his name on top. Check.
Copy and paste it into his email.

> Dear Dr. Zhang,
>
> We are James Murphy, Captain, and Bronwyn
> Barnes, PhD, Chief Scientist, of the NOAA
> research ship *Oceania II*. We hope this letter finds
> you well, and we apologize for the short notice of
> this invitation.
>
> We are writing to you given your recent
> publication, *Population, Development and Marine
> Pollution in China*, excerpted in last month's
> *Journal of Earth Science and Climatic Change*.
> We would like to cordially invite you to spend a
> week aboard the *Oceania II* to share your findings,
> which, we believe, have global implications . . .
>
> . . . *Blah, blah, blah* . . .

The *blah, blah, blah* is mine, because a lot of the science
part of the letter is kind of boring. It has to do with the gyres
that help create these garbage patches. There are also parts
about the garbage vacuum invention thingy Mom and her
team are installing even though they know it's "only a start,
not a cure," and super sad but less boring stuff about the

billions of tons of microplastics that are killing these birds called Laysan albatrosses on some nearby island.

The dead birds part is so awful I google it to see if it's true. I learn how there are tons of them living—and dying from eating garbage—on an island not so far from where we are, right in the middle of this ocean. The chicks are these adorable snow-white fuzzy things, waddling all around, but the mom and dad birds look mostly like seagulls. They live in bonded pairs for up to forty years, unless their mate dies, and then they go find another one. Lots of their mates and even the babies are dying from eating the garbage.

I click PLAY on a video and there's a dude talking, a vet or a doctor or something, and he's opening up a dead one, and its stomach is all full of plastic. Like, literally, so many colorful plastic pieces it would look like an art collage, if you didn't pay attention to it being inside them.

I ex out and return to the rest of Dr. Zhang's letter, which seems even more important now. The next part explains how we want to "welcome you to join us in this opportunity to attract global media attention as a united coalition of scientists demonstrating an unmitigated commitment..."

"We hope," the letter concludes, "the forum will attract

both local and international media, and help share our grave and urgent concern for the health of our world's shared oceans."

At the end, it gives RSVP info and Port of Seattle arrival information, and adds that they'll be joined by students from across the US (which must be the SEAmester kids). It ends, "Together we can make a huge splash!"

I roll my eyes at that cheesy line, then check the name one more time to make sure it's the right guy, copy and paste into his contact form, take a deep breath, and hit SEND.

Whoosh! Gone! Into the interwebs!

A super-proud feeling washes over me.

I tip my chair back and say, "Bingo, baby!" pointing at Captain Jim—well, the photo of Captain Jim that sits on the shelf built into his desk. Which is when I notice something weird, which makes me remember something else.

Captain Jim calling my mom "hon."

Everyone's eyes at the table shooting up at him fast.

Him saying he was only trying to say "honestly." Which now I see was a really obvious excuse.

I pick up the framed photo and pull it closer. It's not just Captain Jim, but the whole *Oceania II* team, standing on deck, the big wide ocean behind them. Blue sky, with nice feathery white clouds.

But it's how Mom stands next to him, her head tilted down on his shoulder, her face happy and kind of weird goo-goo eyed.

And something worse I didn't even see at first.

Something I can't unsee now.

She and Captain Jim are holding hands.

SIDNEY MILLER

Oceania.

Like the ocean in my dream. Like the color of my polish. The same name as the ring toss cardboard boat. The place I got Rachel Carson.

"That's so crazy," I say.

"What is?" my dad asks. He is standing at the stove, stirring a big pot of sauce, or maybe it's stew. It smells like stew. It's his turn to make dinner. Mom and I are setting the table.

I do this a lot. Think something to myself and then say it out loud, and then someone hears me and thinks I am talking to them when I'm not.

"Oh, just the color of my nail polish. Oceania." I hold out my hands, palms down, displaying my blue fingernails, but this time I probably shouldn't have tried to explain.

"You went to a nail salon?" my mom asks.

Uh-oh.

When we finally get that all straightened out, that our excursion to the salon was actually a brainstorming session, it is decided that my terrific idea qualifies as educational, and that I should go ahead with my plan to make a podcast about dreams and dreaming.

First, I have to create an Instapik account so people can find my podcast. I promise my mom that there won't be any identifiable information other than my name. I won't even use a picture of myself, I tell my dad.

So I search around the internet a little for something colorful and eye-catching for my profile picture. Okay, so what is the one thing that everybody in the world is interested in?

Cats, for sure.

Elephants?

Maybe just some clouds in a blue sky? Pretty, but not good marketing.

I need something.

Like from outer space. Or deep underwater

Better yet, something that looks like it's from outer space, but it's from deep underwater.

Like an octopus.

Octopus vulgaris.

The common octopus.

That works.

It turns out to be really easy to find a host site for a podcast. BuzzNet, with a friendly bee icon, gives you a free sixty-day trial, which will take me well past the summer. I figure once I get a couple of hundred followers, I can think about uploading my podcast onto iTunes. After I set up my hosting site, I copy the link and paste it into my Instapik bio: www.SidneyMiller.podcast.net, and I'm all set.

Now, all I need to do is make my first recording.

I think I will do it on precognitive dreaming. People who say they dream about the future, and then it really happens.

That would be so cool.

11.

JEREMY JB "I'LL PROVE I'M NO DUMMY" BARNES

What if this is all a stupid dream? The ship. The photograph with Mom's head resting on Captain Jim. And even everything before that. This whole past year. A stupid dream where Mom and Dad get a stupid divorce, and now we're on a stupid ship and Mom is dating stupid Captain Jim.

But when I open my eyes, the picture is still there in my hand, her head on his shoulder, them holding hands.

I shove it back on the shelf, my mind hopping mad, even though I'm not sure why.

Because, why didn't she tell me? That's why! And this next gross thought: *Is that* why we're here on this ship?

And then another one. The big one:

What if she wants to stay out here with Captain Jim forever?

Last night's dinner blobs up into my throat, making it hard for me to concentrate on my work.

"We're counting on you, JB," Captain Jim said all friendly and nice just an hour ago when I went to the bridge to get his key. "You should be okay down in my cabin now that the storm has passed. Anyway, you slept through the worst of it," he added, laughing. "Which is pretty impressive, I must say. Now let's hope your research skills live up to your sleeping ones."

I thought it was funny then. All chummy. But now anger churns in my stomach. Does he think I'm dumb? So dumb I wouldn't realize he and my mom . . .

Ew!

I cut off the thought and stare at the photo again.

He really must think I am.

My eyes go back to the scientists' names. One contacted, seventeen more to go. I'll show Captain Jim how smart I am. I'll do this right, and get it done. Every last stupid name on the list.

I tighten the motion-sickness bracelets and type in "Ian Agus," which brings up a soccer player, a dentist, and three different Facebook dudes whose pages are private. I remember to add "Australia" and "oceanographer" to the search and—presto!—there he is in Sydney, capital of New South Wales, Australia, author of a study about how changes in oxygen levels are affecting zooplankton.

"Aye, aye, Captain," I say aloud, feeling victorious. "I can't hear you!" Because what else am I supposed to think of when you mention zooplankton?

I find Samara Redmond, deputy director of the International Marine Litter Unit, pretty quickly, and Nicholas Gardner, baseball player, but not Nicholas Gardner Johns, so I decide to skip that dude, since there's a note that I can get more information on him from Marco if I need it.

Next on the list:

- Dr. Sidney Miller—marine biodiversity podcast. Mont Bay Aq.

"Aq" means "Aquarium." I figure this out in a jiffy, so I start on the home page of the Monterey Bay Aquarium. But there's no staff page there. I look back at the list. It also says, "Mind of an Octopus." And "Science Today . . ." next to "Aq"—and that octopus part seems super important.

"Consider the octopus, dude, duh," I say out loud to

myself, because sometimes it helps to talk to someone. "That part is the important part. The octopus."

I add "octopus" to Sidney Miller, with "podcast" too, for good measure, and—voilà!—there he is on his Instapik page, in all his nerd scientisty glory. Well, not him exactly, but a cool pink octopus, which is obviously the avatar for his podcast.

I find that dude's letter with his name on it, double-check that it's the one specifically written for one "Dr. Sidney Miller, Monterey Bay Aquarium," copy and paste that sucker into his Instapik messages, and hit SEND.

SIDNEY MILLER

Six.

Six Instapik followers.

Checking is the first thing I do when I wake up this morning.

My mom and dad. Megan, of course. My aunt Alison. My nana. And Carol Horowitz, the old lady who lives in the apartment next to my nana at the Jewish Home for the Elderly.

A total of six.

"Can you believe that?" I look down into the water where

Rachel Carson is swimming around. She must have just woken up, too, although it turns out goldfish don't sleep exactly. They rest and sort of float around instead of swimming. Besides, they have no eyelids and they can't shut their eyes, so there's that.

"Can you believe it?" I ask Rachel Carson again. I drop some fish food into the water. "Only six. I think I need to step up my game."

Rachel Carson finds the last pellet and gobbles it up. I think I hear her burp, but it's just a tiny ping from my computer that at first I don't recognize. And then I do: It's a notification from my Instapik account. I set it to Popcorn, but the popcorn sounds kind of like a fish burp.

"Maybe another follower," I say. I pull out my chair, sit down at my desk, and open up the app. Still six followers, but in the upper right-hand corner I see a message alert.

"Rachel Carson, we have an Instapik message!"

Dear Dr. Sidney Miller,

We are James Murphy, Captain, and Bronwyn Barnes, PhD, Chief Scientist, of the NOAA research ship *Oceania II*. We hope this letter finds you well, and we apologize for the short notice

of this invitation. We've enjoyed your ongoing
podcast series on marine biodiversity and . . .

Huh?

I read a little more. It mentions "Laysan albatrosses" and
"microbeads" and "gyres." Very interesting, but why is someone writing all this to *me?* Unless it *wasn't* written to me.

I know there are other Sidney Millers out there.

Sixty-four million—in .69 seconds—Google pages of
Sidney Millers.

"Oh, look." I scroll down. "There's one guy from Texas,
a politician or something. And this one's a hip-hop singer.
Whoa, that's so cool."

I turn to see if Rachel Carson is following any of this.
"And there's a Sidney Miller who is a famous actor," I say.
"Well, I never heard of him."

I click back to the letter. It says: *the NOAA research ship.*
That's easy to find. It's a real ship. The *Oceania II,* and it
says that right now it's in the middle of the Pacific.

"Sidney, c'mon. Hurry while they're hot," my nana calls from
the kitchen. "The pancakes are ready."

I can smell them from here, chocolate chip pancakes. My favorite. My parents would never have let me eat chocolate chips for breakfast, but as my nana always says, *Your parents are not here now, are they?*

"Coming, Nana. Just a minute."

Wait, what?

I take one more look at the Instapik message. It says if I—well, if *Dr. Sidney Miller*—accept the invitation, the *Oceania II* will be docking at the Port of Seattle in one week.

Seattle?

I live so close. We drive into Seattle all the time.

The *Oceania II.*

Nail polish. Oceania blue.

The ring toss booth. A plywood ship.

My dream.

And now this?

I have to tell my nana everything. Right away.

It's synchronicity.

What else could it be?

12.

JEREMY JB "ZERO IS NOT SO MANY" BARNES

Chicki, Vance, Henry, Sabira, Marco, Randi, and Mom are all in the mess for lunch, but Captain Jim isn't. Not yet. Which is good, because I'm going to have a hard time even looking at him without thinking of that gross photo.

"Look who's arrived! Our internet king!" Mom says when I walk in, but the title sounds fake and babyish from her mouth, like she's just trying to make me feel more important.

"Hear you've made some great strides," Randi says, squeezing lemon slices into a big glass of what looks like iced tea.

"Not even the storm stopped him," Mom says proudly, forking up a bite of Chicki's homemade coleslaw.

I gotta admit, Chicki can cook. Rumor has it she once cooked for President Obama.

"Good man," Marco says, and he doesn't even sound like he's being sarcastic.

For the rest of the meal, I tell them about how I found the Zhang guy and Ian Agus and Dr. Sidney Miller, oh, and Samara Redmond, but how I couldn't find the Gardner Johns guy, so then Marco gives me all sorts of information about him.

"I've sent out a bunch already," I say, "and I'm pretty sure I'll finish the whole list by the end of the day."

"Even if we get four or five yeses, it would be great!" Sabira says. "Add them to the SEAmester kids and I'm sure we can call it a global summit. And garner some media interest."

Mom nods, eats some more, then asks, "Marco, did you ever reach out to *60 Minutes*?"

"I did," he says. "Not interested. They said they did a story on the Garbage Patch last year."

"Oh, right. One story and problem solved." She shakes her head. "So obvious. What were we thinking, hoping it might be important enough to actually get some consistent attention?"

"Preaching to the choir," Marco says.

"How many other media outlets have we reached out to?"

Marco fidgets around on his phone. "Twenty-seven in total. Mainstream ones include *60 Minutes*, CNN, *GMA*, *Dateline*, *Colbert*, *The View*—" Mom coughs and Marco says, "What? You said you wanted major media attention. They're major media."

Mom nods. "Sorry, sorry. You're right. Keep going."

"Okay, well, and, of course, several trade and scientific journals—Vance did those—and a few local but reputable papers. Oh, and even—and this was Randi's suggestion—*Psychology Today*. They recently did a big story on how fear about the environment is one of the top three stressors in the lives of kids today. From elementary school right up through college."

"Amen to that," Sabira says.

"And how many have we heard back from in terms of confirmations?" Mom asks. "Not that our whole grant extension depends on this last-minute stunt you've all decided on." She looks so sad when she adds that, which makes me think that whatever grant thingy she's talking about actually does depend on it.

Marco stares down at his phone, taps the keys, and scrolls, while the whole room waits on his answer.

"Exactly zero," he finally says.

SIDNEY MILLER

"Well, if it's synchronicity, there's only one way to find out," my nana says.

She drags out the dry-erase whiteboard from the hall closet.

"We haven't used that in years, Nana," I say, watching her open up the stand and set it in the kitchen right next to the table.

"Well then, it's about time," she says.

The whiteboard is where we go to work out any family issues, thoughts, problems, or concerns. My dad will use Venn diagrams, concentric circles, spider maps, you name it. If there is a problem, there must be an answer. Right now, the problem is how to get me—Sidney Miller—on that ship, because the universe is telling us something. And it's our job to listen.

My nana finds the one dry-erase marker that isn't dry, and she waves it around like a magic wand.

"So here we have the goal," she says. She draws something squiggly on the board and makes a circle around it.

"What's that supposed to be?" I ask.

Nana puts her hands on her hips. She says, "It's the boat, Sidney. The research ship. The *Oceania II*."

I say, "Oh."

"Okay, now remember," my nana says, "no suggestion is too crazy. Everything must be considered."

And so that's how we spend the rest of the morning, throwing out ideas, drawing lines from one set of possible outcomes, and then another, mostly coming to dead ends or bad consequences.

Finally, I say, "What's the shortest distance between two points?" I don't wait for an answer, because it's a rhetorical question. I know my nana knows the answer. "Right! A straight line," I say.

So we start over, looking for the most obvious way to get me on the *Oceania II*. A quick Google search and we find out there was an essay contest for high schoolers interested in spending a week studying ocean life and learning about the Great Pacific Garbage Patch.

"If I were in high school and we had known about this before, and if I had written an essay," I say, "and if I had been picked because I had a great essay, then we wouldn't have this problem. I'd just be one of those...what are they called? SEAmester kids?"

Nana jumps out of her seat. "You are a genius, Sidney." She furiously erases the whole whiteboard and hands me the marker.

"To realize your fate," Nana tells me, "takes three things. You've got to want it. You've got to be willing. And you've got to make it happen."

"I do," I say. "I am. And I will."

We plot our idea on the whiteboard, step back, and take a look at it.

"So will you help me, Nana?" I ask.

"I will make it happen," she says.

13.

JEREMY JB "TOO TIRED TO COMMUNICATE" BARNES

"I pretty much found them all," I call to Mom in the bathroom, where she's brushing her teeth. I'm lying on the top bunk in pajamas, ready for bed. "That Gardner Johns guy was easy once Marco gave me the Clean Swell website. I couldn't find the Akilu Bekele, guy, though," I add.

I hear her gargle and spit, and gargle again.

My phone dings, and a bunch of texts from Nicky come in.

How's the Specific O, dude?

???

?????

??????

By the third set of question marks, I realize his texts were sent hours ago.

Sorry! I type back. **Reception is** 🐟🐡🐟 **here. Wet & full o' fish.** The three little dots show up and pulse for a few seconds, but no words come in from him, so I add, **Seriously tho, cool & huge & a lot weird & a little lonely tbh.**

The three dots squiggle again across my screen. **Poor** 👶 **Need a** 🍼 **??**

Very funny, I type back, because I gotta admit, Nicky is pretty good with his emoji game.

Me n the guys will give u lots of 🐥🐥 **huggy wuggs when u get** 🏠. His three dots keep going, then 😃😃😃 and then a whole string of mostly sea-creature emojis 🦑🐙🐢💀👹 appear, then a continual string like he's just hitting anything: a spouting whale, a pair of glasses, another octopus, a spider, a pair of glasses again, a green dinosaur, two girls in black leotards kicking side by side, a green glove, a snowman with stick hands, a bank, a school, the *100* symbol, all making a column down my screen. Finally, the word *Congratulations* appears, which makes fireworks explode.

I laugh, and Mom says, "What's so funny?" so I type back, **Gotta go!** even though I wish I could keep texting with him, because now I'm really missing that dude.

"Nothing, just Nicky telling me something about home,"

I say, tucking my phone under my pillow and turning my head to give her my undivided research-ship attention.

She walks over to the bed and brushes my hair off my forehead and looks at me.

"What?" I say.

"Nothing . . . I just . . . I'm so glad you're here with me." She saves me from more of that by walking away to turn off the light and climbs into the bunk under me. The room is super quiet for a minute. Then she says, "So, it's been almost a week now. What do you think of everyone? Like Marco and Randi and . . . Captain Jim?"

She tries to make that last one sound all casual, but my stomach flips, because what does she care what I think of Captain Jim? Plus, isn't it too late to matter what I think?

"Fine," I say.

"Fine?"

"Yeah. Nice. Good. Funny. Fine. I'm tired," I add. "And I guess I kind of miss home."

"Give it a few more days," she says. "I bet by the end of the trip, you'll love everyone here on board. You'll never want to leave."

I close my eyes, feeling the exhaustion sweep over me. Everything from the puking to the storm to the whole fiasco with the photo and what I think I now know about Mom and Captain Jim. I just want to sleep and not think about it.

At least I found most of the names, sent out the letters. Regardless of what Captain Jim thinks, maybe I'm not so dumb.

"JB?"

I jump a little, just on the verge of sleep. "Yeah?"

"Thanks for all the work you did today. I'm really impressed. I mean it. And we need this. We really do need it. We need this summit to happen, and the press to show up. Without that, there's no way we're getting more grant money."

She sighs deeply and rolls over, her next words muffled into her pillow.

"We're going to need the universe to cooperate. We're going to need a miracle," she says.

SIDNEY MILLER

Making chocolate chip pancakes for breakfast seems like small potatoes compared to what Nana and I have cooked up. Sitting here at the dinner table, I am so nervous I think

I might start laughing out loud, but we have a plan, and a sudden burst of giggles right now would not be helpful.

During dinner, at the mid-salad mark, on cue my nana, who cleverly stayed to eat with us, says, "Sidney, did you ever hear back about that essay contest you entered?"

She's got the best poker face in the world. My nana could have been a great spy, but I can't look at her when I answer, because then I might really start to laugh.

"Oh, wait. You're right. The winners were supposed to be announced this afternoon." I stand up from the table without catching her eye. "I'm going to run and check. Nana, you can tell Mom and Dad all about it."

That wasn't really part of our plan, but I am improvising because I know my nana will do a much better job than I could. Better, I just pop back out with the "big news."

I whisper to Rachel Carson when I'm in my room, "Get ready. If all goes well, we will be going on an adventure real soon."

I count to fifty, and then I head back out to the table. My nana must have killed it because the first thing my dad says is, "So? Any news? Was your essay chosen?" He's so excited.

"I didn't know you had a passion for zooplankton,

Sidney." My mom is gushing. "Tell me more about your essay."

Uh-oh.

I don't know anything about zooplankton.

My eyes widen and I shoot my nana a *what did you do* look, but before I can fully panic, she stops my mom.

"Sidney," my nana says loudly. "Did you find out if you are one of the specially chosen SEAmester kids, invited to spend an educational week on a real research ship in the Pacific Ocean?"

"I did," I announce. "I won."

"Sidney, that's fantastic!" My dad comes around the table to give me a hug, and my mom comes around the other way.

"So can I go?" I am squished between them.

Before they can answer, before they can think too much, my nana says, "I'll take care of everything. Remember, that's my summer job. Secretary of education."

There's a long pause.

And then a big release when my mom and dad look at each other and smile in agreement, and my dad says, "Of course you can go."

My mom turns to my nana. "Mom, you'll make sure she's safe, right?"

"I will, sweetheart. Don't worry. I'll call first thing in the morning and make sure it's all kosher before we even accept the invitation. I know you're both working, so I'll even drive her to the seaport," my nana assures my parents.

"And you'll walk her right up to the dock?" my mom asks. "Make sure she's all checked in properly?"

"Absolutely," my nana says.

NOW, BACK TO WHERE WHERE WE LEFT OFF

14.

JEREMY JB "I GOT THIS" BARNES

The girl blinks up at me. Confused? Grateful? Scared?

How the heck do I know?

All I know is, she isn't leaving and the RIBs are starting to, so covering up my mess feels like the only choice I have.

Otherwise, so much for my expertise.

So my mind is made up: she's Alex Myla-something now. She's got to be.

"Okay, fine. Thanks," she says.

Does this fix anything?

My brain can't think. I just need to let her on the ship.

So we start walking. We are, in fact, walking toward the dock and the RIBs. Me and this girl, and the hippie grandma is running over to whisper something to her, telling her she loves her, then thanking me.

Thanking *me.*

Oh brother.

I stop and turn. I'm thinking I should probably change my mind.

The grandma waves so happy.

"Let's go, JB! Now!" Henry yells. "Marco and Vance are here! They're ready to take you. I can't leave until you're loaded in!"

I blink at him down at the dock, where three gray inflatables idle and SEAmester kids are tentatively climbing in. "All the kids first! JB, let's go!"

We are definitely heading there.

I look at the girl, and she looks, once more, at me.

"Have fun! Be safe!" her grandma calls.

By the time we reach the RIBs, my legs are shaking so bad I'm worried I'll fall in. The girl follows behind. I veer us toward the one Vance is driving. Vance is one of those guys who doesn't pay good attention to much. Luckily, only two other SEAmester kids are already seated on that one, so that leaves room for us.

"Try not to say anything, or even be noticeable," I tell her.

"I can do that," she says, as we straddle the side of the inflatable and climb on.

Early this morning, on the way to port, the RIBs were my new favorite part of this whole science-ocean-adventure-geek-life fiasco, but now, I'm too freaked out to enjoy the awesomeness: the bounce and hum of the boat, the wind in my salt-caked hair, the sea spray splashing back on my face like some sort of fancy spa-facial-gone-mad. Instead, I keep eyeballing Vance's back as he steers, plus the two other real SEAmester kids who are already chatting happily with one another like old pal friends.

I glance at the clipboard in my hand, at the name of the one missing kid—Alex Mylanakos—and now I pull the pen from my pocket and cross it out like they arrived, and work to memorize it the right way, just like I did with the scientists' names.

Myla. Like those shiny silver Mylar balloons that are bad for the environment. No *r*.

And, nakos, like spicy cheesy nachos with a *k* instead of a *ch* sound.

Myla-nakos.

Got it.

I eyeball the girl, hands clasped supertight in her lap, her head down like she's afraid for her life, her knee closest to mine bouncing up and down like a jackhammer.

I lean into her and whisper, "Just stay quiet. I got this. Promise. It's all going to be A-OK."

SIDNEY MILLER

Right before she waved and said goodbye, my nana told me again that I didn't have to go if I didn't want to. She said that the universe didn't hold grudges, and if I changed my mind, it only meant that this wasn't meant to happen.

So, there was this moment when I was standing on the dock and this young guy in a *Titanic* T-shirt was holding out his hand to me so I could step down into the inflatable boat that was supposed to take me out to the massive ship that was about the size of my entire middle school, when all of a sudden, I wasn't afraid.

Not one single bit.

It wasn't anything I could put my finger on. It wasn't all these people, kids and grown-ups chatting away. Or the noise of the outboard motor churning up waves of salty water. It wasn't even the squawking seagulls flying overhead in circles, because in my dream I am certain the birds were different. It was this boy's face. Not even his face exactly, just something about him, and I knew I was supposed to be here. That there was something important going on and that I was part of it.

I put on my life jacket, waved to my nana, and stepped down into the boat. The engine roared up and we pulled away from the dock.

And now I'm terrified.

A lot a bit.

The truth is, I've never been on a boat before. It's thunking against the water, and every time it plops back down I feel it in my whole body, way worse than the Dragon Coaster. Ocean water isn't blue like in the pictures. It's got no color at all except deep.

No one else on this boat seems to be as nervous as I am. The two girls sitting right next to me are whispering to each other like they are best friends. One girl is nodding seriously, the other one is giggling.

The serious one turns to me. "Hey, I'm Diamond." It takes me a second to realize she's telling me her name. "Diamond Blue."

I open my mouth and am about to answer when the boy, the one who checked me in and let me on, the only one here who knows I am *not* a SEAmester kid, coughs really loud like he's about to throw up. He's making all sorts of faces at me.

Oh, right.

When I don't answer, the other girl, the giggly one—I think she is actually wearing lipstick—leans forward and smiles. "I'm Ashley Sperber."

I manage, "Hi," which seems to suffice, because there is no way I am going to remember the name of the kid I'm pretending to be. But the boy is still frantically mouthing something at me that I don't understand, and he doesn't stop until the guy in the *Titanic* shirt turns and starts talking to all of us.

"So, hey, all! Welcome aboard the SS *Vance*! I'm Vance." He laughs and keeps talking, but turns back every few seconds to steer us toward the ship, so it's hard to hear this next part when every few words are lost to the wind.

"My first job is . . . your safety . . . paramount . . . know that number one risk . . . not drowning . . . slip and falls . . . pay attention . . . steps, so seriously . . . life jackets . . . number one focus."

This goes on for a while, until even the two girls start to look a little less enthusiastic. Then the motor stops churning and it gets a little quieter. He goes on, "Listen, this is going to be one of the best experiences you've ever had. You are now part of something really important. Cleaning up our ocean, cleaning up our planet, caring about all life on earth—mammal, bird, reptile, amphibian, fish. It's our job. It's your job."

I'm doing this for you, Rachel Carson.

And I think *maybe* everything is going to be all right. I will certainly be able to report back to my parents about how educational this is. It might even be fun. Then I take a look over at the boy. He's crumpled down in his seat, like he's totally exhausted. He seems pretty miserable, and I feel really bad that it's all because of me.

He seems really nice, actually. Maybe we will turn out to be friends.

15.

JEREMY JB "MAYBE I DON'T GOT THIS" BARNES

"Sorry, sorry!" I say, because I'm shoving the girl into the shower stall in our cabin a little too hard. I pull the white plastic curtain closed to hide her. I open it again.

"Wait, how old are you?"

"Twelve."

"Right. You look twelve," I say. "So, that's a problem. Work on a story."

I close it again.

She opens it.

She looks concerned.

"Like skipping grades?"

"Perfect, yeah. That'll work. And stay here for now. Like, seriously don't move. I'll be right back. Ten minutes, tops, I swear, okay? I just gotta show my face on the bridge."

To be clear, the girl is in our shower in the first place because we lucked out a little, because our RIB with Vance driving was the last RIB to pull up to the ship. And since my brain was super on top of its thinking, I quick told Vance, "This SEAmester kid has to pee super bad," while the other two kids were unloading. "I'll take her to the restroom near the mess and be right back!" and Vance didn't question it one bit.

Now the girl is quiet, doesn't respond, and I can't see her face because the curtain is pulled, and I'm already halfway across our cabin, which only takes six steps, total. So, I take three steps back again.

"Oh, and it's not an actual bridge," I explain, because I don't want her to think I'm leaving the ship. "It's the place where the captain steers from. You'll see. There's a whole welcome party up there."

When I realize what I said, I feel bad. Because who wants to be alone in a shower stall while everyone else is upstairs drinking fancy coconut-pineapple slushies and eating Chicki's mini hot dogs and fancy tea sandwiches?

"I'll bring you a hot dog," I call to her.

The bridge is festive and crowded with our crew plus the scientists who showed, plus the SEAmester kids, all with their lanyards, and seasickness bracelets, and nautical-themed cocktail napkins decorated with helms and oars and anchors waving in the air as everyone talks.

Chicki's two kitchen helpers, Felix and Camilla, are walking around serving bubbly ginger-ale-looking liquid in clear plastic cups.

"Sparkling cider only for the kids!" one of them keeps shouting, pointing to the cups on their tray.

I search for Mom and spot her off in the corner with Captain Jim. My stomach roils because I haven't even had time to think much about all that gross stuff about the two of them with how busy we've all been getting ready for this. Now she looks kind of serious, though, like maybe they're having a fight. Which could actually be helpful, because not so much focus on me.

"Jeremy!" Mom calls, destroying that hope fast. I see her fix her mad face to happy as I walk over. "My awesome scientist wrangler!" She holds out her arm to take me into a half hug and I let her, then wriggle free as fast as I can. "Look at all these global experts. Not bad. Do you see what an amazing job you did?"

Yeah. Amazing. I invited a twelve-year-old who isn't a sci-entist onto the ship.

"Sure," I say, trying to seem casual through the panicked thoughts screaming inside my head. "Anyway, I had to show a SEAmester kid to the bathroom. I should go back and find her now, and bring her back here to the bridge."

"How nice of you!" she says, squeezing me again. "See, Captain? How 'bout this nice, smart, chivalrous kid that I raised?" Captain Jim forces a smile.

I should tell her about the mix-up.

About the girl on the ship.

But, see? I can't. Not with her feeling so proud. And not with *him* here. She'll be humiliated for me.

"I have to go," I say fast. "Find that high school girl and all." I scope around for the server with the hot dog tray so I can swipe a few minis and smuggle them down to her.

"If she gets lost, one of the crew will escort her, honey. You've done enough. Come with me. I want to introduce you to the scientists, and all the rest of the SEAmester kids."

"We're lost," I tell Rachel Carson, lifting her out of my backpack. I set her bag down, cross my legs, and slide down next to her onto the semi-wet tiles. "Well, sure, not lost exactly, since I know we are in a shower stall. But this is not at all how I imagined this going."

A drip of water from overhead lands—*splat*—on top of my head. I look up. Another droplet is forming on the showerhead, and when it gets heavy enough, that one is going to fall on me, too.

"Good point. Okay, okay, so I really didn't imagine anything past getting on this ship. But it definitely wasn't this."

I still don't know the name of the boy who let me on the ship—he didn't tell me—and I can't remember the name of the kid who's supposed to be me. Or, I guess I'm supposed to be them.

I wonder if this is what it's like in one of those movies where a person suddenly shows up and they remember how to do everything, but they can't remember who they are, or how they got where they are.

"I don't know anything." I look through the plastic to the murky water inside Rachel Carson's bag. "But I do know I've got to get you into some fresh water."

When I check my cell phone again, for the seventh time, I've been sitting in here like a bar of soap for twenty minutes. I text my nana: **All good. Keep you posted.**

I really would love a hot dog, but I can't just wait here any longer. When I stand up again, I feel the back of my pants are wet, but I can't worry about that now. I pull back the curtain and peer into the cabin. There are two neatly made beds, and at the foot of each one is a locker, the kind that some girls brought to camp like they were staying a month instead of a week. At least I'm not at camp without Megan.

To the right, no one is there. To the left, still no one. I step out of the shower. Behind me, one more plunk of water hits the tile. I open the door of the cabin and I'm out of here.

16.

JEREMY JB "CUT THE CHITCHAT" BARNES

I have every intention of only saying a speedy, "Hi, yo! Gotta go!" to each of the people Mom drags me to meet, then booking it back down to the girl, who probably now thinks I'm the biggest, worst liar in the world, since it's a half hour easy since I left her. But these SEAmester kids can talk, especially that Ashley Sperber girl (the one who was wearing makeup and jewelry on our inflatable). Plus a dude named Ben Goldman, who's wearing a Bucks Antetokounmpo jersey, so yeah, I'm okay talking to him.

"Milwaukee, for sure," he says, when I ask where he wants to play, because he tells me he's already getting scouted by D1 colleges to play basketball next year.

Who knew you could be super nerdy *and* athletic, too?

"Who do you like for next season?" he asks back, making

me feel pretty cool about a high school dude wanting to talk sports with me.

"Lakers. Or Bucks," I answer. "Or Warriors." He nods, and I wonder if I should ask him the same question in return. But also, I'm thinking, *Enough chitchat, JB, you really need to get out of here.*

". . . same with my roommate, Alex. But I hear he's a no-show . . ." He's still talking, saying, "Kinda bummed about that, because I hear he plays, too."

But now I've stopped dead, panic banging in my chest, because I realize he's probably talking about *that* Alex Mylanakos kid. So she's supposed to be *his* roommate.

"Wait. Who?" I ask, blinking up at him, because maybe I just heard him wrong.

"My roommate. Some kid named Alex. I think we would have hit it off because, according to his Instapik, he's a sports nut, too, but something happened and he didn't show. So now I hear I'm flying solo. Not really terrible, I guess, since I also hear the cabins are really small." He shrugs, but blood is rushing to my cheeks and in my ears. I need to start fixing this now.

"Not a no-show. A *her*," I blurt. "Alex Mylar-nachos. That kid is here. But they must have been confused. You probably were. She's a girl. Um, someone told me that. And then I just met her. So that's probably why she can't room with you . . ."

"Ah, weird. But makes sense," Ben Goldman says. "Wonder wh—"

But I'm already leaving, practically running, because I'd better get out of here.

I race out of the bridge, past the mess and the storage closets, past the library and dry lab, and down the back stairs that let you out right near the schematic of the ship and the laundry room.

I stop and stare at the schematic and breathe hard, thinking.

It always smells good around here. Not like fish, and the endless wet Muck boots. More like breezy cotton freshness and home.

The *Oceania II* laundry room is the cleanest place on the ship. Not fancy, just clean, with two huge industrial washers, and one huge industrial dryer. All of them taller than my head. Plus, it has these cool huge industrial laundry baskets on wheels, filled with clean white sheets and towels.

If Nicky were here, he and me would totally have to race each other around in them.

I walk in and stick my nose down into one of the baskets piled high with folded towels—*ahhh, fresh*—then keep my head in there, because seriously, the clean fresh smell is helping me think.

The real Alex Mylanakos—because, see, now I remember the right way to say it—was a boy. *Is* a boy.

But he's not here now, and the only Alex Mylanakos present is a girl.

A girl, let's say, who skipped some grades and is a high school SEAmester kid.

That's gotta be our story, so we're sticking with it.

I pick my head up and nod, trying to make myself feel sure of all of this, but then I stick it right back down and in again.

Because where on earth is she going to sleep tonight?

That is a good question.

SIDNEY MILLER

Arm & Hammer Sensitive Skin, Free & Clear laundry detergent. I'd recognize it anywhere. My mom and dad use it because it doesn't have dyes, so it's good for people with the allergies I don't have, and because it doesn't have perfumes, so it's not supposed to smell like anything. Except, right now, it smells just like home.

A big whoosh of hot air hits me in the face. I can hear the washing machines running, spinning and whirling and thumping just ahead. So loud. They must be huge.

I keep heading down the hall. It wasn't very nice of that boy to leave us in the shower, but right now I've got to find him, and get Rachel Carson into some fresh water so I can feed her.

"Don't worry," I say. "We got this."

Of course, I really don't, and the smell of Arm & Hammer is getting stronger and stronger, which is making me feel kind of homesick. That must be the laundry room just up ahead. I should take a peek inside; there might be something in there I can use as a fishbowl, and there's probably a rinsing sink where I can fill it up.

"Let's check it out." I straighten my shoulders and head toward where the smell is coming from. Then I stop.

Wait.

What if someone is in there and they ask me what I'm doing?

What if they ask me my name?

I'm still debating the risk/reward ratio, and I think I hear someone inside, moving around.

"Run," I whisper to Rachel Carson.

So we run. I bolt and make a quick right turn at the corner, and then a left. I head down another hall, and when I'm sure I'm far enough away, I stop and lean against the wall to catch my breath.

"I think we just better go back to the room and wait. I'm sure he'll show up." I look down the hall one way and then the other, and it looks exactly the same. I shut my eyes tight and force myself to concentrate. I know I went left. Then straight. Another left. No, right. Then I turned this way. Or maybe it was that way?

How am I going to find my way back to the cabin?

I can't remember at all. And for the first time since this whole thing started, and started to go wrong, I think I'm going to cry. Maybe I read the signs in the universe all wrong. Maybe like my nana said, sometimes it's just not meant to be. Maybe I just have to give up and turn myself in.

I let go a big sigh of resignation and open my eyes, and what I see directly in front of me is a huge map sealed under thick plexiglass and affixed with metal bolts to the wall. It's a schematic of the entire ship, all labeled. The galley. Engine room. Every hallway, like a giant maze.

Wet lab, dry lab—that's cool. Gym.

A gym?

The mess. A lounge. The laundry room.

And there.

A big X that says: YOU ARE HERE.

17.

JEREMY JB "MAYBE I ONLY IMAGINED IT" BARNES

SHE'S NOT HERE!

Here, in our cabin, I mean. Which is where I am now, so I know. She's not in the shower, or under the beds, or anywhere.

Seriously, WTH?

I race backward in my head, like a rewinding movie, trying to figure out if I forgot something, or maybe, better yet, if there never was any girl, and I only imagined it.

There's me, in my brain, back at the schematic.

There's me, back in the laundry room.

Me, before that, back on the bridge.

And me, before *that*, putting the girl in the shower, and telling her to stay.

Stay!

Nope, yep. All of it was real.

But maybe I missed something.

I rewind again. Back to the schematic, which is just a fancy word for ship floor plan, which is where I stopped again, after the laundry room. Because I figured, *Bingo! That might help with where to hide her until I can slip her in with one of the SEAmester girls.*

My eyes skipped down the parts of the schematic: profile, deck, bridge floor, until they got to the stateroom deck. The stateroom deck was the part I care about, because that's where the cabins are.

I tried to slow my eyeballs down, looking for:

Somewhere comfortable.

Somewhere close.

And somewhere safe for her.

My head hurt with emptiness and my eyes kept blinking. Which is why I closed them to think better, wishing I could sink my nose back into that fresh, clean pile of helpful fluffy white towels again.

And voilà! That's when I knew!

Of course: *the laundry room!*

I raced back to our cabin to tell her. And to move her there temporarily.

I burst in the door and raced the six short steps to the bathroom.

But the curtain was open, and the shower was empty.

Holy guacamole!

She's gone.

SIDNEY MILLER

I'm standing here.

"I'm sure this is the right cabin," I tell Rachel Carson. "I'm sure it is."

But now it's locked.

And we can't get back inside.

Maybe crying *is* the right thing to do.

18.

JEREMY JB "EVERYTHING IS BONKERS" BARNES

I try not to panic, but I panic.

Where is she?

I leave the empty bathroom again.

Race back the same six steps to the cabin door.

Yank it open.

And slam face-first into the girl.

Me: (rubbing my nose) Hey! What are you doing? And who are you talking to? And what's that you're holding in your hand?

Her: (rubbing her nose) Getting injured, apparently. And, my fish. Rachel Carson. Wherever I go, she goes.

Me: (feeling bonkers) From the ocean?

Her: No, from the town fair. Goldfish are freshwater fish.

Me: You brought a goldfish with you?

Her: Yes. And she needs a bigger bowl with fresh water. And I need to feed her.

Me: (pulling her into the cabin and closing the door) Let me see.

Her: (holding up the bag) Rachel Carson, meet—Hey, I don't even know your name.

Me: JB. Well, Jeremy, really. But people also call me JB. And, wait. Rachel Carson? Where have I heard that name before?

Her: She's a famous—

Me: Never mind.

Her: Okay. Well, fine. Rachel Carson, meet Jeremy JB. Jeremy JB, meet Rach—

Me: Stop that! I mean, sorry. But we don't have much time. My mom is probably going to be down here any minute. Wondering where the heck I've been. I'm supposed to be—

Her: Your mom?

Me: Yeah. My mom. (I let out a sigh, realizing just how tired I am. How messed up all of this is). Oh, right. You don't know any of this ship stuff, do you? Well, me neither. Not really. Not till ten days ago. But that's why I'm here. My mom. She's the chief scientist on board. Anyway, forget that and focus. We need to focus.

I think I have a temporary plan.

19.

SIDNEY MILLER

You might think hiding in a giant laundry bin would be uncomfortable, but it's really not. Plenty of room to stretch out. The mound of folded towels underneath me are just the right kind of soft but firm. I'm about two feet down from the top, with four canvas walls around me. Even if someone walks in, they wouldn't know I was in here.

I promised Jeremy, because now at least I know his name, that this time I would stay put and wait. He said he'd back with something to put Rachel Carson in and something for me to eat.

"Yes, we believe him. But remember Jeremy? It might be a while," I tell Rachel Carson.

One of the giant dryers suddenly stops, and what I hear is nothing. I think I liked it better before, with the comfortable thumping, thumping. Now I'm listening to see if there are any footsteps down the hall or any voices coming closer.

"All quiet," I say. I decide to take a little peek over the side of my bin. No one in sight. "Guess they're all at dinner."

I roll one of the towels up into a little pillow and lie back down.

"If I was at camp right now, we'd probably be having sloppy joes and bug juice. Oh, no. It wasn't really bug juice. That's just what we called it."

Rachel is resting in her bag of water, so maybe she's asleep already and I'm just talking to myself.

I check the time on my cell phone: 4:55.

Right on cue, my mouth yawns.

My stomach growls.

And that's the last thing I remember.

JEREMY JB "TELL-TALE HEART" BARNES

In English this year, we had to read this scary story by Edgar Allan Poe about a guy who murders this dude with a filmy eye, then buries the body under the floorboards. The murdery guy almost gets away with it, except he keeps hearing the "tell-tale" heartbeat of the dead guy.

"Or maybe it's his own guilty heart he is hearing," Ms. Burnap said, raising an eyebrow at us. "Thump, thump, thump, thump, thump, thump."

Now, walking into the mess for dinner (having left the girl—Sidney/Alex Mylanakos—cozily resting with her fish in one of those giant laundry baskets I took half the towels out of and pushed behind the dryer for warmth), my own heart is pounding like the murdery guy's.

Thump, thump, thump, thump.

I walk to Mom's table. I'm feeling bad enough without seeing Captain Jim sitting there, right next to her.

Thump, thump, thump, thump.

Of course he is.

"Where have you been, JB? Everyone was looking for you."

Thump, thump, thump, thump, thump, thump!

"Fell asleep, sorry. Must've been all the sun at the port."

Wow, the port. *Smart.* How did that even come to me? It seems like a whole hundred years ago.

I sit.

Thump, thump, thump, thump.

"This is Chunbo Cheng...essay winner from New York City...Diamond Blue...Chicago...Dr. Samara Redmond...Marine Litter Unit...Ian Agus..." Mom keeps talking, introducing me to people I've mostly already met, at least briefly, up on the bridge earlier, but I can't keep my brain focused because it's racing all over the moon. Plus, my eyes are frantically searching around the room for good containers to put someone's goldfish in. Finally, I get my eyes to stay back at our table for a second, where we're all mixed together: crew, scientists, and SEAmester kids.

Thump, thump. Thump, thump.

My ears focus on Mom's words, which are still saying names and stuff.

"How-dee-doo," I answer, coughing. Mom gives me a weird look. I pick up my glass and chug water.

"Jeremy is the one who did the hard work of inviting you all . . . ," she's saying now. Then she holds up a glass to toast everyone.

"You need help, don't you?" the Diamond Blue girl sitting next to me whispers.

Huh?

"I can tell you're lying. I know when rescue is needed."

I turn and blink at her. Did I imagine her just saying that?

She smiles and keeps her voice low. "Your face, kid. It says it all. Beet red. And your knee is bobbing so hard it's making me more seasick than this ship."

I open my mouth to say something—anything—but she cuts me off.

"Shhh, come to the buffet. I'm starving. I'll help you while we load up. Who can't recognize when a kid is lying to his mom?"

We return to the table with so much food heaped on our plates, I get strange looks from Chicki and Mom. But we just kept loading while I spilled what I could of the mess I've made to Diamond Blue. She swore secrecy, and I trust her. I don't know why, but I do. Plus it feels good to have help. I may be in over my head.

"We're very hungry," Diamond Blue says, sitting. "Everything looks so amazing."

She may be some sort of superhero.

"So, can I have everyone's attention?" Captain Jim asks, standing and tapping his glass with a spoon. For a second, the *thump, thump, thump* ramps up again. But he's just making a toast. It's obviously not about me.

"As you can imagine, we are endlessly grateful for your commitment," he's saying, "but what you should also know is that the future of our mission is in jeopardy. So, in addition to your important input and ideas on how to best clean up our oceans, the point of this summit is to garner some much-needed media attention. Because attention means money, right?" He rubs his thumb and first two fingers together. "And money allows us to continue the work. So maybe Vance will update us on how many news outlets have RSVP'd with interest so far. Since we have a whopping six days before our big trip to what we call Albatross Island. You'll soon see why we call it that." He winks here. "And fluffy baby birds eating copious amounts of garbage, you'll agree, is our best chance at the kind of flashy story that will really interest reporters."

"Yeah, Vance," Marco says. "How many media RSVPs?"

The room grows uncomfortably quiet.

Sabira coughs.

"No firm ones yet," Vance says, deflated. "But no fear, we're still trying."

"And we've got some new leads," Sabira adds hopefully. "More like scientific outlets, though, than major news outlets."

"Oh, and the *Sacramento Bee*," Vance says, sounding cheerier. "I forgot them. They've got good readership and said they'd send someone out to cover it if they can." Mom's face perks up a little, but Sabira pokes Vance in the side and shakes her head. "Oh, right. My bad," Vance adds. "They said only online," and Mom's hopeful face sags down again.

When Mom speaks, finally, her voice shakes.

"I don't understand it. This work we're doing is important. Critical. Since when is the death of our oceans not a big enough story? What do they want, flying fish? Magic beans? Dancing babies? Oh, I know. Cats, right? Cat stories are all the rage." She stabs a broccoli spear with her fork like it's the enemy. "If it were some stupid gimmicky story, it would go viral. They'd cover it till the cows swam home."

"Cows don't swim," Captain Jim says, sitting back down

and squeezing her shoulder, not even trying to watch what he's doing in front of me. "Let's try to enjoy what we do have, for now. All of this." He takes his hand off her shoulder and motions around at the scientists and SEAmester kids, but then puts it right back where it was, and this time Mom is too upset to even notice his public display of affection. I try not to notice, either, or to pay attention to whatever the heck is going on between them. I can't worry about that now. I have way bigger problems to solve.

Speaking of which, Diamond Blue leans over. "I'm going back to my cabin to shower and rest. Cabin 12. My room-mate is her. Katie." She nods at a super-tall ginger-haired girl. "We'll figure the rest out among us girls. Good luck, JB. Keep cool. And see you at midnight," she says.

SIDNEY MILLER

Rachel Carson is tucked right next to me, safe and clean and well-fed and swimming around in the iced-tea dis-penser Jeremy brought back with him from the kitchen, along with a plate of mini hot dogs and a root beer. Well, Rachel Carson isn't swimming around with root beer and hot dogs. Those were for me.

Jeremy seemed pretty proud about his elaborate ruse for sneaking out of his cabin after dinner, telling his mom he was going to the game room to play video games with someone named Henry, and then how he told Henry he was going to bed early with a headache, even though he doesn't seem like the kind of kid who gets headaches. I have to admit it was pretty clever. I am starting to think we would make a pretty good spy team.

"You know, my mom would probably be more upset about the dinner I had tonight," I tell him, "than the fact that I'm a stowaway on a ship in the middle of the Pacific Ocean."

I can't see him because he's hiding in his own laundry bin right next to mine, but I hear Jeremy give a little laugh.

I am staring up at the tubes winding around along the ceiling. I guess he is, too. "Those look like worms from a horror movie," I say.

"Yeah, they do," Jeremy answers. "*Invasion of the Expandable Exhaust Ducts.*"

Jeremy told me we have to hide and wait here until the SEAmester girl shows up at midnight and sneaks me into her room. That's the latest plan.

"*Return of the Fifty-Foot Dryer Monster.*"

I know mine's not so good, but Jeremy laughs anyway. *"Night in the Zombie Laundry Room,"* he says.

Then we're quiet for a beat. It's not completely dark in here. There's a row of tiny lights along the floor, but they just cast an eerie shadow. I pull myself up onto my knees and peek out over the top.

"That one was a little scary," I say.

I see Jeremy's hands, and then he appears from inside his bin. "Yeah, you're right. Sorry. So hey, why would your mom be mad about your dinner?"

I tell him a little bit about my mom and dad and how they worry so much about me all the time, but basically they are pretty cool. And he tells me how his parents separated last year, and how, just last week, he saw a photo of his mom holding hands with—jeez, really?—the captain of this ship we are on right now.

"That's got to be hard," I say.

He looks away and just kind of shrugs, and I know that weird feeling when you've just told someone you barely know too much about yourself. So I try to change the subject. "What time did she say she was coming?"

"Midnight."

My backpack is propped up right next to Rachel Carson's iced-tea dispenser. I pull out my cell phone. "It's almost twelve now," I tell him.

"Is it? I hope Diamond Blue gets here soon, before my mom wakes up and realizes I'm not in my bed." Jeremy swings his feet over the top, hauls himself up backward, and drops down to the floor. "Whoa," he says, righting the basket, which almost toppled over.

"How do you know we can trust her?" I ask him. I'm getting dizzy watching him pace back and forth.

"I'm pretty sure she's legit," he says. "Anyway, she offered, and we need her." He takes a bunch of steps away from me toward the entrance, leans out into the hall, turns his head left, then right, then walks back toward me. "Hey, all that stuff you told me about your grandmother and everything," he says. "I've been thinking about that, and thinking, maybe you're right. Maybe some things are just meant to happen?"

"I don't know."

"And that word you used," he says. "About something sinking?"

"Synchronicity?"

"Oh yeah, that. Synchronicity. What is that about again?"

So I tell him again, as best I can. About the nail polish, the fair, the ring toss, all the garbage littering the ground, Rachel Carson, and about my dream.

"And of course that invitation I got," I say. "By mistake. Just out of the blue like that. Right on my Instapik. I mean, I don't even have any followers. So how do you explain that one? Right?"

Jeremy's face turns red and he starts fidgeting.

"That was *you?*" I ask.

And he tells me. Everything. How important it was for him to get that right. About his really smart older brother and sister, who are twins. About how he got responses from so many of the scientists. About the pink octopus on my profile, which also seemed right for a marine biologist. And how he found . . . well, *me.*

"So that's why you had to let me on? So your mom wouldn't find out that you messed up?"

Jeremy nods. "Pretty stupid, huh?"

"Or," I say, "it was the smartest thing you ever did. Maybe we're here because we are supposed to be here. Maybe the two of us are supposed to do something really important."

I can feel my heart start thumping really fast, like it's beating outside my chest and I can hear it. "I just know it."

Jeremy presses his hands together and brings them up to his lips, like he's thinking really hard, and then his eyes suddenly light up. "I think I know exactly what that is," he says.

And so Operation Code Pink Octopus begins.

OPERATION CODE PINK OCTOPUS

- DB EXPLAINS TO KATIE (WHO SEEMS COOL :)).
- DB LETS SIDNEY/ALEX IN HER ROOM.
- DB COVERS FOR SIDNEY AT ALL TIMES.
- JB GOES TO SEAMESTER LABS, TOO, TO NOT MISS IMPORTANT DEVELOPMENTS. THIS WILL MAKE HIS MOM HAPPY ANYWAY.
- SIDNEY AND JB HAVE CODE PINK OCTOPUS LUNCH MEETINGS / LAUNDRY ROOM. FOCUS ON SAVING MISSION!!!
- HOW THEY DO THIS IS GET MORE PUBLICITY!!
- HOW THEY DO THIS IS ???????????

TOMORROW

20.

SIDNEY MILLER

I didn't get to sleep until after midnight, but I wake up before the other two girls. As quietly as possible, I take my dream journal out of my backpack. I start to write before my dream slips out of my brain.

But too late.

"What are you doing?" Diamond Blue is sitting up, rubbing her eyes.

Katie Feinstein is still sleeping, tucked into blankets, curled up like a little cat on the floor between the two beds. She insisted. She said after a month of camping in Israel, indoor mattresses were too soft for her.

I shut my notebook. "Nothing," I say. They already know I'm not in high school like they are, but I don't want them to think I'm babyish, writing in a diary. One with sparkly shark stickers on it to boot.

"Well, I write in my journal every day," Diamond tells me. "Marie Curie kept one, you know."

"So did Albert Einstein." Katie pops up without skipping a beat. "Hey, I hear your goldfish is named Rachel Carson," she says.

I nod. "I hope it's okay I keep her here." The iced-tea dispenser Jeremy gave me is working really well. There's lots of room for her to swim around in, and the top has this little opening for air, but I can snap it shut if I need to move her in a hurry.

Diamond swings her legs out of bed. "Are you kidding? Who better to have with us than one of the most famous women scientists in the world?"

Could this actually be exactly where I belong?

But then, just as I'm thinking this is all going to be okay, I might just be able to fit right in, Katie gets up.

"Diamond, you can shower first," she says.

She is an Amazon.

Katie bends down to gather the bedding, and when she stands up again, I think she's got to be almost six feet tall, with messy red hair that looks twice as big as it did yesterday. No one is ever going to believe we are both in the same grade.

"Thanks." Then Diamond gets up and reaches for a folded towel from a metal shelf over the only other piece of furniture in the tiny room, a desk bolted to the wall. She's so short, shorter than I am, she just barely grabs it.

Okay, whew.

So maybe, just maybe we can pull this off.

"Okay, after me, then you can . . ." Katie turns to me. "What's your name again? I mean, what's your name supposed to be?"

Diamond pauses at the door to the bathroom and listens.

"Um . . . it's . . . I think it's . . . Alex something," I start. Jeremy must have told me a million times last night in the laundry room, but now I can't remember.

And the three of us are all looking at one another. I think Diamond starts to laugh first. Or maybe that's me. But before you know it, we're cracking up.

Like we are friends.

My mom would be happy.

Come to think of it, I am, too.

JEREMY JB "OFFICIAL-SOUNDING STUDENT SWAPPER" BARNES

The problem with Code Pink Octopus, and especially bullet number three of Code Pink Octopus, which says that Diamond Blue will cover for Sidney at all times, is group assignments—specifically, SEAmester kids being broken up into Groups A, B, and C—meaning Diamond Blue isn't necessarily assigned to the same group as "Alex Mylanakos," aka Sidney Miller.

I find this out because of Code Alert text #1 that comes in from one Sidney Miller at 0700 this morning.

CP 🐙 Alert: Not in DB group! OMG! Help!

Stay put! I type back. I got this!

It takes me exactly three minutes and thirty-eight seconds to get from our cabin (dressed with teeth brushed) to the dry lab, which, if I do say so myself, isn't half-bad. Can't speak for the condition of my hair with its poking-out pieces.

Sidney waves tentatively when she sees me, eyes bugged wide, waving hand glued unobtrusively down at her side.

Clearly we haven't thought this all the way through.

Not only this problem with group assignments, but

how young Sidney looks standing outside the dry lab next to the other SEAmester kids who are *not* Diamond Blue, all of them waiting to go in. Why Sidney has decided to stand next to Ben Goldman in particular (she's like a sapling standing next to his giant oak), Jordan Delgado (who already has a freaking mustache), and lipstick girl Ashley Sperber (hey, maybe it would help to put some of that lipstick on Sidney, too!) is a big question.

But no time to ask it or worry about that now because my cell phone buzzes, so I'll have to remind her later.

I yank it out of my pocket.

It's her.

Sidney.

Code Alert text #2.

CP 🐸 Alert: Now what?

She grimaces.

NP, I type back. **Gimme a second. I'll figure out a way to fix it.**

I fly into the dry lab, where Randi (my least favorite choice of crew researchers, since she always seems ready to catch me doing something wrong) is setting up stations with markers and graph paper, and big yellow envelopes that read, *Water Sample Testing and Logging Methods.* Each kid's name is written on an envelope in black Sharpie with their group letter. I scoop up the one that reads, "Alex Mylanakos."

"Sorry, she's with me!" I say, waving her envelope at Randi's face, so close I'm hoping it makes it hard to see. I also snatch up Randi's clipboard with the group assignments. She looks at me, perturbed, like she doesn't even know what I'm doing here. Which is fair enough, since I haven't set foot in the dry lab once since I came aboard.

Come to think of it, now that I look around, I should have. It's pretty cool in here, if I do say so myself.

There's a semicircular desk the size of like six desks all glued together, with computers at each person's space. The same image moves around on each screen—a shot, I'm pretty sure, of the underneath of the visible edge that starts the Great Pacific Garbage Patch. You can see nets dripping with seaweed and gunk, and foggy water clogged up with those microbeads, and also a metal cylinder that must be equipment because it's marked *Oceania II.*

Stretched across the entire far wall is a map of the Pacific Ocean and the spot we are in (which I know because it has a big red circle that says YOU ARE HERE, and also shows Hawai'i and California and even the Golden Gate Bridge).

The center is labeled North Pacific Gyre, and three big arrows point to currents flowing in three different directions that somehow push the garbage to this pile.

"JB, give me that! What are you talking about?" Randi pries the clipboard from my hands.

I look away from the map and back to Randi, and I think fast.

"There's this Alex girl," I say. "She's super shy. Like I mean *super* shy. And . . . allergic to things. Yeah, that. So many things. So, my mom says she should be with her roommate at all times, Diamond Blue. *All* of the time. Because of the shyness and allergies. Um, *needs* to be. So I have to swap her. Okay?"

Randi gives me a suspicious look and says, "Are you sure, JB? Or maybe *you* just want to be with her . . ." She winks at me.

Great.

So now she thinks I'm busy trying to arrange romancey things.

I'm about to protest but remind myself I can't really worry about that now. I have to keep sounding official. Get the job done.

"Yeah, so, no. It's just . . . I'm stepping up around here,

or hadn't you heard? I'm Mom's right-hand man at all times now."

Randi actually blows one of those spit-take laughs like, if she were drinking, she would have sprayed liquid all over the room.

"Fine, right-hand boy. Kid. Whatever," I say. "Right-hand *son*. But don't question her. My mom. Okay? Because she doesn't like that. Just know that I'm trying to be of optimal assistance around here." I bow, making an at-your-service loop-de-loop with my hand. Randi rolls her eyes, but it works, so who cares? She hands the clipboard back to me.

I scroll for Diamond Blue's name.

Phew!

There she is. Group B.

"Put her in Group B," I say, sounding super confident, in charge of things now. "The Alex M. girl, I mean. You could just swap her out for . . ." I breeze down the list again. "Nadji Stewart. Put her in Group A, and we'll be good as new," I conclude.

"You're sure about all this?" Randi asks, still kind of smirking. I nod emphatically, avoiding eye contact. "Okay, then."

She searches through her pile of Group B envelopes for

Nadji Stewart's one, crosses out her B and writes A, takes the Alex Mylanakos envelope from me and crosses out the A and writes B. "Satisfied?" she asks. I nod. "Great. Now, put this one back where you took that one from."

"Aye, aye, Captain," I say, saluting her.

She rolls her eyes again.

"And just so you know," I call to her, as I rush out of the dry lab and back toward Sidney, "I'm gonna put in a good word for you and tell my mom she should probably even give you a raise."

I add some finger guns for emphasis, which is a pretty nice touch if you think about it.

SIDNEY MILLER

Once I'm off the hook and safely back with my co-conspirators, I can breathe. I'm not sure what getting caught at this point would look like, smack in the middle of the Pacific Ocean, though I'm pretty sure they don't have a jail or a brig or whatever they call time-out on a ship. But they'd definitely call my parents, and even if I could take the punishment, I don't want to get my nana in trouble.

"Eh, they'd just make us walk the plank," Jeremy says. "Can you swim?"

"Funny."

I think he's feeling a little too confident about how he handled my SOS text, but I can say I'm impressed myself. I got dismissed and sent to meet up with Diamond and Katie's group. Now we're waiting our turn in the dry lab for the instructor. I think her name is Randi.

"*Kinda* funny," Diamond says. "But seriously, maybe we should all exchange cell numbers in case something like that happens again."

"Agree. And we need some kind of hand signals. Like in baseball." Katie nods. "Yeah, and maybe like a getaway plan, too."

"Get away from what?" I ask. I'm not liking the sound of this. Maybe they do have a brig on this ship.

Jeremy looks like he is about to say something, but the door to the lab swings open and music blares. Lady Gaga is singing "Bad Romance." A split second later, a woman in shorts and hiking boots walks in and right past us. She's got a lanyard around her neck that reads S. REDMOND.

"Oh, I'm sorry," the woman says aloud but to no one in

particular. Quickly she pops her earbuds into her ears and plugs her phone in. All our heads turn to follow her, as she picks up a laptop from the long metal table and walks out again.

Jeremy lifts his chin proudly. "Hey, I invited her. All the way from the UK, which stands for United Kingdom, not ukulele," Jeremy says. "Pretty cool, huh?"

Whatever he's talking about, I am not paying attention. "Get away from what?"

There are signs posted everywhere in here. Taped to the beams and tacked to the walls.

MAKE SURE TO CLOSE AND LOCK DEEP FREEZER.

DON'T LEAVE THE COFFEE MACHINE ON.

EMPTY YOUR OWN COFFEE FILTERS.

EXPERIMENT IN PROGRESS—DON'T DISTURB.

Diamond gives Katie a warning glare. "We don't need hand signals *or* a getaway plan. All we need to do is not draw attention to ourselves."

"That's right," Katie says. "Everyone just calm down."

"Right, we just need to keep a low profile." Jeremy crosses his arms, and his elbow bangs into what looks like a giant microscope and a petri dish labeled HEAVY (BROWN-TIPPED) STARFISH. We all watch, sort of frozen, while the whole thing wobbles a few times back and forth, then decides to tip toward the edge of the counter.

Diamond comes to her senses first, snaps her hand out, grabs the top of the microscope, and steadies it again. We all exhale at the same time.

Phew.

But the petri dish has slid in the opposite direction, because, you know, for every action there is an equal and opposite reaction, and is now sailing down toward the floor.

"Oh no," Diamond says.

Katie holds out her palm and the plastic container lands perfectly. "Fly ball." She smiles proudly.

We exhale in unison.

"Whew, that was a close one." Jeremy steps back away from the counter, and it looks like he is going to lean against the wall behind him, except it's not a wall. It's a projector screen, and behind the screen is a flimsy-looking folding table with about a dozen glass beakers.

"Wait, stop," I shout out.

Diamond gasps.

Katie actually screams.

Jeremy balances on his heels, his arms stretched out and

rotating in frantic circles for what seems like minutes but is probably only half a second, before I grab him and he's standing upright again.

The microscope is still on the counter. The starfish is still dead in its petri dish. The screen hasn't tipped over. The glass beakers are safe. We look at one another with wide eyes.

"Okay, now. One more time," Diamond announces. "What is it we need to do?"

"Keep a low profile," Jeremy says. He puts his hand out. "On three."

"One," Katie says. She does the same.

"Two." Diamond puts her hand over Katie's.

"Three." I lay my hand on top of the others.

When we lift our hands into the air and call it out, we are, I am certain, a pretty good team.

THE NEXT DAY

21.

JEREMY JB "BOSS OF THINGS" BARNES

"I could do it," I say, grabbing at the clipboard Mom's trying to hand to Randi for RIB assignments. Because apparently SEAmester groupings get changed every day. Just to make my life more difficult. "Sorry, rude, I know," I say. "It's just . . . it's a good job for me. And I like helping out with these things." Randi watches me suspiciously. "Plus, I like to be the boss of things," I add, not just laughing but throwing my head back like I'm completely hilarious. Which works because when bossiness doesn't, humor always does.

Mom hands the clipboard to me.

"Sure, why not?" she says. I quick scan the SEAmester names.

"Okay, right. So . . ." I pause and act thoughtful, like I need to think hard about groupings. "Kenneth, Christopher,

Jordan, Chunbo, and Barak with Marco," I say. "And Ben, Katie, Diamond Blue, and Alex Mylanakos with me and Vance. The rest with you, Mom. Good?" I lean into her and whisper, "I left you the smartest ones."

Everything goes smoothly with boarding, and like that, we're zipping out on the open water and the stress of the last twenty-four hours and Operation Code Pink Octopus melt away.

Ben sits next to me on one side, Sidney on the other. Katie and Diamond Blue sit across from us. Ben and Katie are tall, tall, tall, and both look like full-grown adults. Luckily, Diamond Blue is short and skinny. Next to her, Sidney doesn't look so out-of-place young.

Sidney glances at me and smiles. "So far, so good," she mouths.

I smile, too, close my eyes, and relax for the first time in days, losing my thoughts in the cool, salty ocean spray.

SIDNEY MILLER

It is nothing like my dream at all.

The Great Pacific Garbage Patch.

I've read about it. I watched a Nat Geo special with my dad. But here, I never imagined anything like this. This can't be right. This can't even be real. This can't possibly be our planet, the one that is rotating on its axis while it is revolving around a giant plasma ball.

The one that is perfectly in balance, a closed system, a hydrological cycle of rain, rivers, clouds, sun, the ground, the sky. The ocean.

Because every drop of water we have, all of it, circles around, evaporates into the sky, and comes back down as rain, or mist, or snow. It sinks into the ground and fills rivers, ponds, lakes, reservoirs, and the well in my backyard.

Water I shower with. Cook with.

And drink.

No new water is ever made.

This is all we've got.

In my dream, I could see right into the water, down to where it went from blue to green, where the light from the sun broke the surface and shot down like laser beams. Was this really what was supposed to happen? Did the universe want me to see *this*?

I look over and catch Jeremy's eye. A second ago he was smiling, but now he's not anymore, and I know he's thinking the exact same thing. What could two kids, a boy and a girl, possibly do to fix this? A thousand people could come out here on an inflatable boat like this one, and every single person could pick up a hundred pieces of garbage every day for a year, and it wouldn't even put a dent in what we are seeing now.

"I think I'm going to be sick," Ashley says. She puts her hand over her mouth. Diamond looks like she's about to cry, and Katie already is.

It isn't until Vance, the guy in charge of our inflatable boat, starts to talk, that any one of us can breathe again.

JEREMY JB "CRACKER JACKS" BARNES

If you want a RIB full of teenagers to shut up fast, bring them way close up to the edge of a floating garbage pile that's bigger than the state of Texas. Garbage and junk as far as your eye can see.

I'm a joking sort of guy, but there is nothing funny at all about seeing it up close.

Vance gives us facts, like how the Great Pacific Garbage Patch is really two patches connected by, like, a superhighway of garbage, and it covers over 1.6 million square miles of ocean space. It contains more than 1.8 trillion pieces of garbage and weighs at least 88,000 tons, the equivalent of five hundred jumbo jets.

"And that's just the stuff that's collected here," Ben says.

"Right? Like it's really spread out throughout the whole ocean. Most of it, you can't even see."

Vance nods and says, "You'd think we're getting a handle on it, but these new numbers I'm sharing with you are actually many times higher than previous estimates. And they keep going higher."

"It's so, so sad," Katie says.

"And disgusting," Diamond Blue adds, reaching out to squeeze Katie's hand.

"You sure can feel the urgency of it all when you see it up close," Ben says. "What if it's too late to try to fix it now?"

"It can't be. Humans made it, so we need to fix it. End of story," Vance says. "Oh, man. Look at this." He leans over the side of the RIB and scoops up what looks like a small fisherman's net, except it's full of garbage, and several dead fish. "Don't any of you do what I just did," he says, meaning how he leaned over the side. "It's actually against the rules, but I couldn't just leave this in there. At least it's a teaching moment." He tosses the net on the floor of the RIB, and we all just stare. I spy more dead fish, a small yellow rubber duck, a comb, three toothbrushes, a bunch of those six-pack plastic holders that go around the tops of cans. Vance shakes his head. "They're called ghost nets because fishermen abandon them, toss them overboard. This is only a small one. In the larger ones, we've seen whales caught up . . . whole ecosystems . . ."

His voice trails off and we're all quiet, staring in disbelief at what's right in front of us, when you focus your eyes around the seaweed and rope and kelp: a laundry detergent bottle, Twinkie wrappers, shampoo bottles, disposable razors, a baby doll head, and a thing that looks like a gray Pokémon ball. Also, red plastic cups, three light-blue face masks with elastic earpieces, and a surgeon's see-through yellow rubber gloves. And last but not least, a mostly mangled Cracker Jacks box, though I can still see part of the baseball and the sailor guy, plus the letters *Cr* and the whole word *Jack,* and who even eats those anymore?

"Cracker Jacks," I say quietly. And that's when it hits me.

A memory I have, which loosens an idea that was forming in my head as I tried to fall asleep last night. And the name of the guy. I was trying to remember, but I was afraid to tell Sidney. But now I'm sure.

Jacks.

Something Jacks.

Daniel. David.

No.

Damian.

Damian Jacks.

That was his name. The dude with the puffy black hair I saw talking on the news a few weeks ago with Grammie and Pops while we were eating dinner. The one who was doing a story on some high school kid who had discovered a supernova.

"Kids," he'd said, pointing at the camera, like he was pointing right into my kitchen. "Mark my words: kids and our youth. That's who's going to really help change things. I really believe this, and I'm willing to put my cameras behind it. They are smarter and more capable than most of us give them credit for. Kids, not adults, are the future of our planet."

22.

SIDNEY MILLER

You worry about the lab, I'll worry about Damian Jacks. That was the first thing Jeremy told me when we got back to the ship.

But now it's a whirlwind. Apparently, the samples we just pulled up from the water with the rosette need to be rushed inside to be processed as soon as possible. And *apparently*, they can get contaminated by *us*, by our hands and clothing.

"So *we're* the contamination problem?" Barak mumbles.

"Of course we are," the girl named Nadji says.

Vance gives out directions. "You guys stay on the bridge and clean off the equipment. Jordan, Ashley, Diamond, Ben, and . . . what's your name?" Vance points to me.

"Alexis Mylanakos." Jeremy rushes forward and trips over the metal gangplank-looking thing lying across the ground. "Alex. We call her Alex."

Vance does a double take. "You look a little young," he says, but then he doesn't wait for an explanation; besides, Jeremy has already taken off. "Okay, you five are with me. Grab the cooler. And let's go."

There's some confusion over who is supposed to be carrying what, and it all looks really heavy. Two boys wind up lifting the cooler and lugging it inside. We all have to walk through a gym, I mean a *real* gym, to get to the wet lab, and I know instantly why they call it that. Let's just say, it's a good thing the floor is all rubbery.

All the scientists—aside from Dr. Sidney Miller, of course—are hunched over a long metal table in the center of the room. Most of them are wearing earbuds or headphones, so they don't even notice us crowding in a circle around them. It's not that big in here.

There are pumps swooshing. Water whooshing. When one of the scientists, the one with long hair and a colorful beanie on, gets up and walks over to a giant freezer, it makes a loud sucking noise, and frosty air pours out.

Vance starts talking.

"What happens next is called processing. All the water samples we just gathered need to be filtered. The rosette has gathered water from different depths. Every ten meters. Does anyone know why we do that?"

There are computer monitors everywhere. One seems to be a video stream from the bridge, one shows a weather map, another is turned to a soccer game. There is what looks like a giant microscope on a table under the round windows at the other end of the room. And everywhere, taped to the walls and even the huge metal girder I'm leaning on, are safety signs. What to do in an emergency.

I count four fire extinguishers.

My dad would be pleased.

"Anyone?" Vance repeats the question.

Diamond and Ben both raise their hands, but Ben doesn't wait. "Because the salt content is different the deeper you go."

"True." Vance nods. Still none of the scientists even look up.

"And it's colder.

Behind me, Ashley shouts out, "And it's colder."

"Yes, but what does that mean?" Vance asks. "Diamond?"

"Just how far down the plastic particles go," she answers. "And how much of it gets into our food chain." Diamond lowers her head. "And how many sea animals we're destroying by throwing our garbage into the sea."

JEREMY JB "TWEETING LIKE A CHAMP" BARNES

@CODEPINKOCTOPUS

Hey @DamianJacks What do a goldfish, blue nail polish, a bunch of SEAmester kids, 8 scientists & 1.8 trillion pieces of garbage have in common? Bring your crew to the Midway Atoll, Nat'l Wildlife Refuge, bright and early this Friday to find out! Can't-miss story of the century!

@CODEPINKOCTOPUS

Hey @DamianJacks Supernova schmoopernova. Meet two 12-year-olds trying to help save the oceans! Bring your crew to the Midway Atoll Nat'l Wildlife Refuge, bright and early this Friday to find out! Can't-miss story of the century! P.S. Don't worry. There are adults here too!

@CODEPINKOCTOPUS

Hey @DamianJacks Roses are red, violets are blue, 88,000 metric tons of garbage are waiting for you! (So come help us save the planet!) Bring your crew to the Midway Atoll Nat'l Wildlife Refuge, bright and early this Friday to find out! Can't-miss story of the century!

@CODEPINKOCTOPUS

Hey @DamianJacks Why did the chicken cross the road? To get away from a garbage pile twice the size of TX. We are the chickens. Never mind. Just bring your crew to the Midway Atoll Nat'l Wildlife Refuge, bright and early this Friday to find out! Can't-miss story of the century!

@CODEPINKOCTOPUS

Hey @DamianJacks Put your money where your mouth is. We're kids helping to save the planet. Share our story! (We're so getting grounded once you do, so please make it worth it.) Midway Atoll Nat'l Wildlife Refuge, bright and early this Friday to find out! Can't-miss story of the century!

Sidney finishes reading and blinks up at me.

"You sent all of these?"

"Yeah. Good?"

She laughs a little. "Really good, Jeremy. Tweeting that guy like a total champ."

THE NEXT
FEW DAYS

23.

SIDNEY MILLER

You'd think as a science geek I'd be good with numbers, but I'm not. I would always count the kids ahead of me in class, then look ahead in the math book to figure out which problem I was going to get before I was called on.

Hoping to control one of the variables.

I tried to do the same with the seating assignments in the mess for dinner. Katie figured out that they were arranging where everyone sits using last names—Mylanakos, not Miller—and counting by threes, in order to mix things around and make sure everyone gets to know everyone else, and not just the kids in their group.

But I must have, of course, done the math wrong.

Because unexpectedly, tonight, I get put at Captain Jim's table, and we all know that grown-ups, especially moms, ask a lot of questions. The captain's table is where head scientist Dr. Barnes always sits. Jeremy's *mom*, Dr. Barnes.

"So, Alexis, is it?" Captain Jim reaches his hand out to me.

I smile. "Yes, sir."

I avoid catching Jeremy's mom's eye when I take the shake, which is hard since she's sitting right next to him. A little close, if you ask me, but maybe I just think that, since Jeremy told me about that photo. And how it bothered him.

I get that.

"I hear good things about you, Alex."

It's Jeremy's mom.

This up close, she's even prettier than she was from far away. She's not wearing any makeup, and her hair is pulled straight back into a ponytail. I bet she's really nice, too, but the last thing I want to do is talk to her and slip up.

They are going to call us up to the buffet by table so there's not a long line. If I can make it until it's our turn, then eat really fast, I'll probably be okay.

"Mylanakos," Jeremy's mom says to me. "That's such an interesting last name. I went to grad school with someone with that name. Is it Greek?"

I want to look over to Jeremy for help, but he got put

at another table and they've just been called up to get their food. He told me it was chicken potpie night, and he said it was the best chicken potpie he'd ever had, and I was really looking forward to it because the food on this ship is actually really good.

But now I just have a twisted stomachache.

"I'm sorry, Alexis," Jeremy's mom says. "I hate when someone does that to me. Like there are only two Mylanakoses in the world and you must be related to the other one." She smiles. She really *is* nice.

And I feel bad that I'm lying to her.

"It's okay." I've rolled and unrolled my cloth napkin four times.

I don't even know exactly what would happen if anyone found out who I really was, but now there are bigger things to worry about than Rachel Carson and me being stowaways, like saving the planet

I've got to remain incognito for just a little bit longer.

"So, I know I should remember this," Jeremy's mom goes on. "But which essay was yours, Alex? I couldn't read all of them, of course, but I did read a fair number. They were all so impressive. You kids never cease to amaze with your passion."

I open my brain and hope it starts working.

I didn't know you had a passion for zooplankton, Sidney.

And I take a chance.

I mean, what choice do I have? It looks like Jeremy is still heaping chicken potpie and ambrosia salad onto his plate.

"That's just what my mom said when I told her I was writing my essay on zooplankton," I say, looking straight at Jeremy's mom.

The best way to lie is to tell the truth.

24.

JEREMY JB "YOU CAN TEACH AN OLD FISH NEW TRICKS" BARNES

Sidney, Rachel Carson, and I have gotten pretty good at our stealth lunchtime Code Pink Octopus meetings behind the large laundry bin we keep pushed behind the washers and dryer for optimum cover. During the day, the whir and hum of the machines is so loud that even if Camilla or one of the other crew members comes in, they probably wouldn't even hear us.

It can get kind of warm back here, but it's the price you pay for security.

The first thing we do each day is update Code Pink Octopus with completed and new information. I'm here first, so I go ahead and change it while I'm waiting.

OPERATION CODE PINK OCTOPUS

- ~~HOW THEY DO THIS IS GET MORE PUBLICITY!!!~~
- ~~HOW THEY DO THIS IS...~~????????? DAMIAN JACKS!!!
- ~~TELL AS MUCH TRUTH AS POSSIBLE AND DON'T GET CAUGHT.~~
- ~~JB TO TWEET THAT GUY DAY AND NIGHT ON HIS TWITTER TILL HE ANSWERS.~~ WAIT FOR DJ TO ANSWER.

The second thing we do is share stuff about our day while giving Rachel Carson some good friendship and attention, speaking of which, here Sidney is now, clutching Rachel Carson in her iced-tea dispenser. It's looking pretty cozy and snazzy in there. We've already added some fake plastic seaweed and a scuba diver plastic action figure I found and suction-cupped to the bottom. You can find everything on this ship, even suction cups, if you look through enough drawers in the mess room or dry lab, I'm telling you.

Today I have a new surprise for her tank, which will only add to the festivities.

"I made her a gift," I announce as soon as Sidney gets close enough to hear.

"You did?" She looks pleased.

"Yeah. I already updated our CPO list, so I'll show you. But first, it requires some explanation."

I jump up and run over to the laundry bin, where I've stashed things, and fish out the large white Styrofoam drifter buoy me and the other SEAmester kids decorated this morning in Randi's Group B.

"I don't usually like art projects, but this one was pretty cool," I tell Sidney. "They each have our name on the front." I turn my buoy from its back, decorated with a decent enough Sharpie shark swimming through waves, to the front, where it says, *Jeremy JB "Science Is Pretty Cool" Barnes*. "Oh, and get this. They have a GPS embedded so we can literally track them from our phone as they track the currents. You'll be making yours with Diamond Blue and the rest of your group this afternoon. In the morning, we'll all toss them overboard together in a ceremony." I'm talking a mile a minute. Sidney keeps nodding, trying to keep up.

"So, anyway, see here?" I turn the buoy on its end and point to a small, perfectly round hole in the bottom about the size of a large cherry. "This is where the *drogue* will go. That's like a pole that acts as an anchor and keeps the buoy moving with the current through the water. That's how we'll track where the garbage drifts and stays for the next several months. Later on, the crew will go out and collect them."

Sidney nods some more and finally says, "And that's Rachel Carson's gift?"

I laugh and shake my head. "Oh, no. This part is."

I reach into my pocket and fumble for the small Styrofoam ball that came from the place we made the drogue hole. It's kinda rough, but I worked hard to smooth it better with some sandpaper. Then I drew the four black lines across it with a thinner Sharpie.

"Sadly, no orange paint to make it look super official," I say, holding it out to Sidney.

She takes it, then looks at me. "You made her a basketball?"

I nod, proudly, reaching into my other pocket for the tiny plastic desktop basketball hoop I found suctioned to a wastebasket in the game room. I hold that out to her, too.

"What are we going to do with those?" she asks.

"Teach Rachel Carson to shoot hoops!" I say, lifting the lid carefully off the top of the dispenser. I push the hoop below the surface and press the suction cup against the wall.

It stays pretty well. I take the ball back from Sidney and drop it in. It bobs nicely along the surface. "Now she just needs a teeny-tiny Antetokounmpo jersey," I say.

"You're ridiculous, but funny," Sidney laughs, "but I'm pretty sure you can't do that."

"Put a jersey on a fish?"

"Yes, that, too," Sidney says. "Or teach her to play basketball."

"Actually, you can," I say, feeling smart. "Me and Nicky—that's my best friend—once spent a whole night watching Instapik pet-trick videos, and there was one of some old lady who taught her goldfish to do all sorts of things." Sidney looks at me suspiciously, but she's interested. "Maybe it was a betta fish and not a goldfish. But that can't matter too much. Can it?" Sidney shrugs. "Anyway, it looks good in there, right?" She nods. "Okay, so, now hand me some food."

"For what?" she asks.

"Her first training lesson." Sidney rolls her eyes, but she retrieves her fish food bottle from her pocket and sprinkles a few pieces in my palm. I pluck a single piece and hold it near the ball and move it toward the hoop until she swims after it, bumping the ball once, probably by mistake, with her nose.

Sidney laughs, but with the next piece, it seems clear that Rachel Carson definitely bumps the ball as she chases the food.

"Let me try!" Sidney says, and by the sixth or seventh piece, Rachel Carson is actually kind of pushing the ball across the tank and near the hoop.

"Score!" I yell, satisfied, and Sidney busts out fall-over-laughing now.

When she composes herself again, she seems more determined than before, so she's busy feeding Rachel Carson flake after flake of food in front of the ball, when the little red notification on my phone pops up.

"Sidney," I say, tapping her excitedly. "Look!" I thrust my phone in front of her very concentrating face so she has to stop and see.

"Look what?" she asks, pushing it away.

"Stop. I'm serious. This is even better than a goldfish trick."

She finally stops what she's doing to look. "What is th—?" she says, her eyes going instantly big, as she realizes. "You mean . . . ?"

I nod hard. "Yes! Who else?" The notification is in our Twitter @CodePinkOctopus message box.

"Okay, wait. Hold on. Hold on." She drops the rest of the fish food in her hand into the tank and squishes down next to me, breathing hard.

"Ready?" she asks.

"Yeah, I think so. Ready."

"We read it together. So, go!"

We hold our breath as I move my thumb to the little blue birdie icon and click onto the site.

📷 @DamianJacksCNN

@CodePinkOctopus Interested to hear more! Please email my producer Gin Maroney @gmaroneyCNN with details ASAP. Thanks!

WHO CAN KEEP TRACK OF THE DAYS ANYMORE?

25.

SIDNEY MILLER

There is a real porthole in our cabin, with the cover propped open, and moonlight shines in like a giant flashlight. I kneel on my bed and peek out. The darkness goes on forever, so you can't tell the ocean from the night sky, except for the stars like dots against the black. I've never seen so many stars in my life. I wish Megan could see this. I reach under my pillow to get my cell phone to take a picture. I start my text:

Hey, Megan.

Miss you like crazy cakes. 🍰

So much is happening out here in the middle of the Pacific Ocean. 🚢

2 much to put in a text.

But just know if you don't hear from me when this week is over, it's because I'm in liar jail.

But before I push SEND, I think and I stop myself.

Wait.

What time is it in Hong Kong?

First, I need to know what time it is here.

My cell phone says it's eleven fifteen p.m. I'm wide awake. I'm thinking about everything that's happened and what's, maybe, about to happen. It feels like just this morning I was on the dock with my nana, and it feels like a hundred years ago.

Like I belong to both places at the same time. The way it happens in a dream.

I concentrate hard and do the calculations. In Hong Kong, it's two fifteen.

Two fifteen p.m. Two fifteen *tomorrow* afternoon. Just thinking this hard hurts my brain. But whatever way, whatever happens, and by whatever time that would be for Megan, Jeremy and I will know if our plan worked.

I press SEND.

I see text bubbles bubbling right away. I hear a ping, and Katie shifts around a bit in her sleep. Diamond lets out a sleepy sigh. Quickly, I turn off my sound. I slip under the covers to read Megan's reply.

Liar jail?!

What did you do now?

That's a good question. Where would I even begin?

I impersonated a famous scientist.

I falsely accepted an invitation that I knew was not meant for me.

I made my nana an accomplice in a huge lie to my parents.

I lied to my parents.

I snuck onto the research ship *Oceania II*.

I hid in a laundry bin.

I lied to the head scientist on said research ship.

I impersonated some kid named Alex Mylanakos.

I endangered my goldfish.

I poke my head out of the covers and look over at the desk, where her iced-tea dispenser is secured behind the convenient shelf brackets that are everywhere on this ship.

"I know, I know, Rachel Carson. You wanted to come."

I'll explain it all later.

I better get some 😴💤

Tomorrow is the big morning of

Wait.

I stop typing. I delete that last line. I attach my photo I took out the porthole, which I now see is just a black round circle, but I send it anyway.

I don't want to jinx anything. If all goes well, if *anything* goes well, Megan will get to see it on TV.

JEREMY JB "SOMETIMES YOU GOTTA BUG" BARNES

Between SEAmester activities, secret Code Pink Octopus meetings, drifter-buoy launch celebrations, and ship-time meals, the days are flying by quicker than a remote control fast-forwarding boring old commercials on superspeed.

Damian Jacks or not, tomorrow is the trip to the Midway Atoll wildlife refuge. I can't sleep, but clearly Mom can, because she's snoring in the bunk below me.

I slip my phone out from under my pillow where I stashed it and click on the Twitter icon and my messages to make sure I didn't read Damian Jacks's response to us wrong, after I gave his producer more of the details.

📷 @DamianJacksCNN

@CodePinkOctopus Sounds interesting, but very short notice, so I make no promises. But I'll see if we can scrounge up a crew. If we miss you this trip, give us a heads-up on your next mission.—DJ

It's pretty darned nice, but that last line worries me. Without Damian Jacks, there is no next mission. I quick type that back to him, hoping I don't bug him too bad, then listen to Mom sleep deeply some more.

She's happy out here in the middle of the Pacific Ocean. Tired, but happy. The happiest I've seen her in a long, long time. And the work she does is really important. I don't think I got how important before I actually came out here and saw it with my own two eyeballs.

I click on messages and start to type one to Nicky.

Hey, dude. Can you believe I've been out to sea so long?

I try to think of what else funny and sarcastic I can tell him, like how stupid it is out here, and how bored I am out at sea with a bunch of geeky annoying science people.

But it's not. And I'm not.

And, actually, they aren't.

Even the ones who are, really aren't.

Lots to catch u up on, I type instead, wondering how I'll ever truly explain even the half of it.

THE BIG
MORNING OF

26.

JEREMY JB "STILL A GOOD JOKER" BARNES

By the crack of dawn, we're loaded into our RIBs, same assignments as last time, which means me, Sidney, Diamond Blue, Ben, and Katie together, but this time with Mom driving, not Vance. Our boat is at the front of the fleet, or whatever you call a group of inflatables.

"Hey, what do you call a group of inflatables?" I suddenly ask Sidney, smiling, because even during serious times, it's good to have a lot of joking left in you. She narrows her eyes at me, thinking, then shakes her head. "A rack of RIBs," I answer, laughing, and despite her nervousness, she laughs, too.

"That's a good one," she says. "Now, focus. This is it. Code Pink Octopus or bust."

And of course, she's right, but I'll still have to remember to tell that one to Nicky when I get home.

We're quiet again, and her knee bobs up and down. We may be the only nervous ones. All the other SEAmester kids seem excited, but they're not waiting for Damian Jacks to appear.

Or worse, to not appear, and the mission to end, and everyone from the *Oceania II* to be sent packing home.

I can tell Mom and the crew (but not Captain Jim, who had to stay back with the ship) feel the weight of it. They seem mostly quiet and deflated.

"We can't lose sight of the good we are doing, just because there isn't someone to document it to the world, Dr. Barnes," I heard Sabira tell Mom early this morning as we loaded supplies into the RIBs. Mom kissed Sabira's forehead and said, "I know. I do know. And, you're right, of course. I'll just miss everyone . . . and wish the world would care more about facts and science than a media circus."

Now, as the RIBs' motors start up and we head out, and the anxious chatter quiets, I'm thinking, *What if me and Sidney actually manage to deliver at least a bit of media circus? What if we fix everything?* Then I slap those thoughts down, because if he was coming, wouldn't we have heard something from him this morning?

I reach in my pocket to double-check Twitter messages on my cell phone, then remember I don't have it with me. "No phones today," Mom told everyone. "Not even for photos. You can find plenty of great photos on the internet. Today is about being present."

A few kids groaned, but most of us nodded and agreed, including me, which means *What is actually happening to me out here?*

I'm lost in these thoughts when Mom suddenly turns around to face us.

"We have a bit of a ride till we reach our destination," she says. "So, who here can tell us something about the Midway Atoll?"

"I can," I say, my hand shooting up without my permission. Diamond Blue laughs, because I guess it's not like a classroom where you have to raise hands. Mom's face looks shocked.

"Well, great. Go ahead, then, JB," she says. "That would be wonderful!"

"An atoll is a round island or coral reef, maybe, with a

hole or lagoon in the center, that got formed around a volcano, but now the volcano is long gone."

"Wow, excellent," she says, surprised, but I'm not even done, because I am still a pretty decent internet expert who did lots of researching last night while she was snoring—research, I might add, I smartly messaged to Damian Jacks.

"So, a bunch of servicemen used to live on the Midway Atoll, because they were actually stationed there during World War II. There are no servicemen there anymore, but there are still military bunkers, plus white sands, and lots of birds and a bunch of other critters and seals."

Mom smiles and says, "That's excellent, JB. Share more, please, would you? And discuss. But amongst yourselves. I need to concentrate for a bit here." She pulls out a walkie-talkie, and then she's talking to Vance and Marco about directions or knots or something.

I close my eyes and lean my head back, feeling proud, as the air starts to lighten and the sun starts to come up, and everyone is busy oohing and aahing at stuff I'm almost too sleepy to see, and my mom, the chief scientist, steers us smart science SEAmester kids toward a white-sand island far off in the distance, just becoming visible across the calm morning waters of the Pacific.

SIDNEY MILLER

My mom had me go to these yoga classes last year when she thought I was too stressed at school. I believe they call that a *projection*. Like when your mom gets cold and then she tells you to put on a sweater.

Yeah, like that.

But if she could only see what I am seeing now, she'd never have to make me do yoga again.

What I see:

Orange.

Orange but also red, like I've never seen before, not like the flame of a candle, but like a leaf in the fall hanging on a tree branch still alive.

Yeah, like that.

Like the sky is alive.

The sun comes up from behind the clouds, which float like giant balloons. And a ball of fire is resting on the horizon, practically shouting at us, telling us to pay attention.

Diamond leans over and whispers to me, because without saying so, everyone has stopped talking. "It looks like heaven would look, doesn't it?"

It does. But I'm not sure if I say this aloud or not.

None of us on this trip has been awake and outside this early before, to see a day just as it is beginning. It feels like it's happening too quickly, in fast-forward motion.

Before we can even fully take it in, the sunrise is almost gone.

It is as if we can actually feel the earth turning, as if we could see the arc of the globe in its entirety, from the very start of time to now.

And then we all startle when a fish leaps out of the water. And then another. They are shiny silver with big round eyes and wings like birds, spread out wide. One disappears and another follows it.

"Flying fish," Jeremy's mom says softly. "Aren't they beautiful? Sit quietly and we will probably be visited by a family of white-sided dolphins."

Nobody moves.

It is just Katie, and Ben, and Diamond Blue, and Jeremy, and his mom. And me. And the whole Pacific Ocean.

27.

JEREMY JB "WHAT IS HAPPENING HERE?" BARNES

I open my eyes to bumping and sloshing and Mom yelling loud and serious, "JB, everyone, sit up, look alert! It's rough over here. I don't need anyone going overboard."

Straight ahead is the island, poking up just a few football fields in front of us. The water around us is fairly shallow, all whitecaps and turmoil on top of some of the most clear turquoise water you've ever seen. Gray dots cover the island. Ben, across from me, points and says, "See all of those? Those are the Laysan albatrosses!"

Mom stays quiet and focused, her stance extra wide, trying to keep herself upright as she begins to swing the RIB around toward the shore edge part of the island.

I turn to Sidney, embarrassed that I crashed like that,

missing most of the ride, but her face is distant and nervous, and maybe the slightest bit green.

"Are you okay?" I ask, leaning in. "Worried about Damian Jacks?"

She turns to me. "No, not that. It's just, the waves . . . I think I'm going to be sick."

SIDNEY MILLER

I have never thrown up in public before, and I do not intend to now. I think maybe I should have paid more attention in yoga.

Breathe.

Just breathe.

Better yet, maybe just splash a little water on my face? I feel dizzy. Voices flood in from behind me.

Whoa, hold on.

Getting bumpy, guys.

We're almost there.

Hang tight, rough waters.

The boat goes up like a skateboard doing a wheelie, and

then down like an anvil dropped from a skyscraper. *Thud.*
I feel it in my teeth.

And the next thing I know I'm not in the boat anymore.

I'm in the water.

I mean, overboard, in the ocean.

Before I can figure out what just happened, a gulp of salty water hits me, *splat*, in the face. I clamp my mouth shut, but it's too late and a gulp goes down my throat.

I can't feel the ground.

Where am I?

My life preserver floats up and presses into my chin. My clothes are sticking to my arms and legs so I can't move, and my sneakers feel heavy.

I twist around but I don't see the boat. I don't see anyone. I see water. I paddle frantically with my arms and legs and all my strength, but I'm not getting anywhere.

How can that be?

Where is everyone?

Then it happens so fast, I'm not sure of the order of things.

Diamond grabs the straps of my life preserver and drags me up to the side of the boat.

Katie, who has clearly panicked, shouts out, "Oh no! Somebody get her. Get Sidney. I mean, Alex! I mean . . . Her real name is Sidney. She's friends with JB, or, like, a stowaway or something. She's not even a real SEAmester kid!"

28.

JEREMY JB "UH-OH, DOUBLE UH-OH" BARNES

Diamond Blue is tiny but strong, and she has Sidney gripped tight by the life jacket before Ben is even up on his feet and on our side, reaching down. He's the one who hauls Sidney up out of the water and back into the RIB.

"You okay?" Mom calls as she steers us out of the deeper swells toward the white-sand beach of the island.

Sidney coughs and shivers a little, but it's only when Mom turns to me, her eyes filled with fury, that I realize the full extent of what Katie just said.

SIDNEY MILLER

I almost wish I *had* thrown up in the boat instead of sitting here sopping wet. It's so embarrassing. I must have looked so stupid bobbing up and down in the water like a human buoy, because I leaned over the side just after Dr. Barnes told us all to sit down and needed to be saved like a stupid little kid. Like a middle schooler.

But worse than that.

Way worse.

Jeremy's mom looks like she's about to blow a gasket.

I have a very bad feeling that I've just ruined everything.

29.

JEREMY JB "WOMANING UP" BARNES

The rest of the RIBs are pulled up on the beach next to us. Marco, Randi, Henry, Sabira, and Vance unload supplies as the scientists and SEAmester kids disembark on both sides. Everyone is happy and excited and chatting loudly. Everyone except the people on our boat.

Ben climbs out first, followed by Diamond Blue, but as Katie starts to make her move, Mom stands in front of her, says, "Sorry, kiddo. Not so fast."

Katie's eyes dart apologetically to me, then to Diamond Blue, whose eyes dart apologetically to Sidney's, whose dart apologetically back to mine.

"Alex," Katie says softly. "I meant Alex. I really did." But it's too late.

"Someone want to explain to me what's going on?" Mom says, fuming.

Katie babbles something about being so scared she didn't know what she was saying, and Diamond Blue begins a convoluted story about how Sidney is Alex's real first name and her middle name is Alex, but she likes that and hates Sidney, and she isn't even sure what Katie was saying about that whole stowaway thing.

Mom's mad face is going back and forth, back and forth, between the girls, until finally Sidney, looking small and scared and drowned-rat wet, steps up.

"They're just being nice, Dr. Barnes. Trying to help me. To, um, cover. This is all my fault. Not JB's. But it's true. I'm Sidney Miller, not Alex Mylanakos, SEAmester kid. I just needed to be here because of . . . Well, I guess not needed but wanted . . ."

And while she goes on about nail polish and her best friend, Megan, who moved away, and the horrors of summer camp, and about her nana and grandpa, the grandpa she never got to meet, and how their love story proves *blah, blah, blah* about synchronicity—all the same stuff she told me that day at the port—I keep my head down and eyes averted. I can't look at Mom's face and see how mad and sad and confused and disappointed she is.

And yet.

I can't *not* look, either.

And worse, I realize, I can't let Sidney do all the explaining. I can't let her be the only one to man up.

"It wasn't all her fault," I say, pushing up next to Sidney, so I can woman up instead. "It was my fault. I invited her. By mistake. I invited the wrong Sidney Miller to our ship. I was embarrassed and didn't want you to know. Or Captain Jim to know. All she did was accept the invitation. Because of her dream and her grandma, and her goldfish."

"Goldfish?" Mom interrupts, shaking her head, but I plow straight forward.

"But I invited her. And I'm the one who snuck her on board." The whole rest of the story rushes out, from her octopus avatar and podcast, to more about her nana knowing and okaying it, and the weird stroke of luck about the one missing SEAmester kid. When I finish, I add, "So now you know how stupid I am. Because that's what I am, Mom. Stupid, with a capital *S*. And I know you always want to pretend I'm smart like Sean and Sammi are. But I'm not and I never will be. I'm a dope. The dumb one. Jeremy JB 'I'll Always Be the Stupid One' Barnes. You know it. I know it. And now everyone on the whole entire ship will know it. This proves it. So, yeah."

I gulp back a feeling that threatens to turn into tears.

Sidney takes my hand and squeezes it. "That's not true, Jeremy. You are smart. Very smart. More than you know. I don't care what anyone says."

My mom closes her eyes, then opens them again, then opens her mouth to say something, then closes it again. Then she shakes her head, and opens her mouth and closes it again. She's trying not to say something she'll regret, but she looks like Rachel Carson eating her food.

Finally, she says, "Do you understand, Jeremy? Do you *know* the trouble I could be in? We could *all* be in? It's not—it's not a smart or stupid thing, it's a liability thing. There are laws, rules, waivers, protocol . . . Do you know how dangerous this was?"

"Sorry," I say, *sorry* because now I see it, me, for what I've done. Instead of saving the mission or helping my mom, I've only made everything worse.

I wait for her to say more, but I can tell she's trying hard not to. Not to call me names. Not to yell at me in front of everyone. Not to say how disappointed she is.

Finally, she looks up, all Chief-Scientist-Barnes business. "Katie, Diamond Blue, you go join the others. I'll catch up in a minute. And tell Marco I need him. I can't have her out here another second." She nods at Sidney before looking straight at me. "I can't have *either* of you out here right now. We have work to do. *I* have work to do, and this may be my one last shot. Even if no one will ever see it or know. So I'm staying here, and you two—you two—are going back. Marco's going to have to take you both back to the ship."

30.

SIDNEY MILLER

A helicopter.

What else could it be?

We all hear it at the same time, me and Jeremy and his mom standing in the wet sand by the boat, Katie and Diamond Blue a bit away, looking at us with worried faces, and all the rest of the SEAmester kids and scientists, and Marco and Randi and Vance, who have gathered farther ahead under a white canopy tent.

But everyone looks up in the sky at the same time, hearing it long before we can see anything. The thumping rhythm, blades slapping against the air, and the engine's steady churning coming closer, and getting louder.

It has to be.

"A helicopter," I whisper to Jeremy.

"A helicopter," he whispers back to me.

It's bright red, a giant insect with one huge glass bug eye, white lettering stretched along its side: CNN NEWS CHOP-PER. The sand it kicks up makes a mini tornado, stirring everything up like an eggbeater. It lowers down at an angle, the tail end tipping upward, and hovers just above the water.

Thud. Thud. Thud. Thud.

It lands.

Thud. Thud. Thud.

The whirling begins to slow.

Thud. Thud.

Thud.

Before the blades completely stop turning, the door slides open and a woman with a camera perched on her shoulder spills out. I don't think either Jeremy or I have taken a single breath yet.

"You did it," I say.

"We both did," Jeremy says back to me.

"What?" his mom asks. "What did you two do?" But she is staring straight ahead, not looking at either of us, as someone else steps out of the helicopter and makes his way toward us. I don't move my eyes, but in my peripheral vision I can see everyone rushing back.

Vance is shouting. "Do you see this? Do you see what I'm seeing? Is it? Is it really?"

"No way. How did this happen? How did they know?" Randi is the fastest. She's way ahead of everyone else, calling out, while a whole trail of high schoolers lope across the sand, trying to catch up.

"It's really him, isn't it?" Marco says. He's huffing and puffing when he comes to stand beside Jeremy's mom, and we are all looking in the same direction.

"It is," she says. "It really is. It's Damian Jacks."

31.

JEREMY JB "WHO DA MAN NOW?" BARNES

Up close in person, Damian Jacks looks like a cartoon dad. Tall, tall, tall, like makes-Katie-and-Ben-look-short tall, with chiseled cheekbones, a jutting chin, thick black hair that's blown back from the slowing whir of the helicopter blades, and the biggest, whitest smile you've ever seen. That dude could do toothpaste commercials.

He wears khaki shorts, a green polo shirt, and Timberland work boots that leave sizable footprints in the wet sand. His camerawoman is short and stocky, with short-short blond hair, and the camera is almost as big as she is.

Sidney and I stand frozen, our mouths open, watching them move toward us all, as Damian Jacks looks around.

"What a crew you've got here!" he remarks. "Glad we

made it. Global summit, indeed. But where are my two superstar kids?" He scans the crowd of us, crew and scientists and SEAmester students. "I want the twelve-year-olds who reached out to me. The ones who insisted I come."

There's a confused murmur from Mom and Randi and the crew. Then Sidney raises a tentative hand from where we still stand glued by the side of our beached RIB. Mom turns and gawks.

"You did this, Alex?"

"Well, Sidney," Sidney whispers. "And it was way more JB than me."

Mom falls into step with Damian Jacks, who beelines toward us, nudging away Marco, who was just prepping the RIB for our departure. He shakes our hands, hard, and winks like a secret message to us that he totally gets Code Pink Octopus.

"Ready?" he asks, indicating that the rest of the crew should gather around. "We're about to go live." Then he maneuvers Sidney and me to either side of him and slings an arm over each of our shoulders.

We face the camera with him.

"Smile big," he says. "*Everyone*." Then to his camerawoman: "On three, Sandra, okay?"

ONE CRAZY HOW-IS-
THIS-EVEN-HAPPENING?
INTERVIEW

"Are we on?"

The camerawoman nods, and Damian Jacks taps on his mic just to be sure.

"Great. Hello, viewers! Damian Jacks here, coming to you from the Midway Atoll today, a national wildlife refuge located on the far northern corner of the Hawaiian archipelago, one of the oldest atoll formations in the world." He gestures across the white sands and around to the edge of the ocean, then returns his focus to the camera.

"This atoll is a nesting habitat for millions of seabirds, including the Laysan albatross, *Phoebastria immutabilis*, a gull-like population, now gravely threatened, not by natural prey, but by human waste and consumption."

"He means garbage," the boy, JB, pipes up, leaning boldly toward the mic to clarify. "Let's call it what it is, because kids my age? We want to get it. To understand it. And then we want to fix it. And these birds—and fish—are dying because of miles and miles of garbage."

"A thousand miles," the girl, Sidney, chimes in. "The

Great Pacific Garbage Patch is literally twice the size of Texas and constantly growing. So not really so *great* at all."

"Really, we're just two kids. The scientists are the ones who can explain it best," the boy says. He motions to a young woman in a pale green silk headscarf decorated in sea turtles and starfish and whales.

Crew member Sabira steps up. "It's amazing how many people still don't know how much waste—garbage," she corrects herself, "is floating out in the middle of the Pacific."

"And there are at least five of these piles. Five!" a young man wearing a GARBAGE IN, GARBAGE OUT T-shirt adds. "You only have to be human to understand that it's crushingly sad."

The camerawoman pans wide, moving from the white sands, to the shallow turquoise waters, to the vast blue ocean, the beauty of it masking approximately 88,000 tons of garbage—just one of five garbage islands humans have allowed to accumulate. As if on cue, a murmuration of graceful gray-white birds swoops in, landing in the sand. Among the flock, a mama bird and babies, three white fluff balls of feathers so cute they make one's teeth ache, waddle toward the crowd. The camerawoman pulls tight in on them before panning back to Jacks again.

"How cute," Damian Jacks says, squatting to get closer, the camera moving along with him. His face shifts to concern, as a few more waddle into the shot. "And to be blunt, from what I'm told, in a few short months, too many of them will likely be dead. Because these birds are dying at an alarming rate. Why? Because of *us*. Is that right, Dr. Barnes?"

"That's right." The woman who serves as the *Oceania II*'s chief scientist sweeps a wisp of hair off her face as she squats next to where one of the babies has wandered up to her, practically on her foot. She doesn't try to touch it or pet it, just lets it move there in the protective shadow of her bent knee. "We want people to know about this particular species because they—and this island, this spot—are a microcosm of what's gone wrong in our world. Thousands of these beautiful creatures are dying each week, in a wholly avoidable way. Death by garbage. By *plastic*."

"But not if these two preteens can help it," Damian Jacks announces, standing again and ushering the boy and girl forward to come stand by his side.

"This is Jeremy Barnes, Dr. Barnes's son, and his friend Sidney Miller, both seventh graders who, one short week ago, didn't even know each other. Now, through some pretty crazy coincidences, they say they're the best of friends. It was their idea to bring me here to the Midway Atoll. It's quite the story, actually." He laughs. "When you hear it, you're not going to believe it. But it's not only true, they have a name for it."

The girls squeezes the boy's arm, leans in, and whispers something excitedly to him.

"They're calling it 'synchronicity,'" Damian Jacks continues, looking to the kids, who nod. He holds his phone in front of his face and reads from it. "What psychologist Carl Jung called 'meaningful coincidences,' and maybe it is. Whatever it is that brought them together, and us all here, to learn and grow? We're calling it change, and hope for the future."

THE MIDDLE OF
THE NIGHT . . .

32.

JEREMY JB "SHARING IS CARING" BARNES

"JB?" Sidney whispers. "You in here?"

I barely hear her above the whir and hum of the dryer loud in my ears from back here. The floor under me vibrates in the dark. I shine my phone flashlight up like a beam guiding a ship.

It's past midnight. Everyone else is asleep. Well, everyone except whoever's on watch on the bridge.

Shhh, I text. Back here.

I couldn't sleep. Not a chance. Not after all the excitement of the past twenty-four hours, and knowing that in fourteen short hours, we'll actually be saying goodbye. Hard to believe I care so much, when I just met her one brief week ago.

But I do. *Care.*

Besides Nicky, I think she may be one of my best friends.

CP 🐙 Alert!! I had texted her twenty whole minutes ago. Laundry room. Our spot. Stat! I've been waiting here, tucked in towels, ever since.

One last Code Pink Octopus meeting.

I reach behind me and shove the gift I wrapped in the 79 AU 196.97 T-shirt deeper into the pile of terry. It's digging some into my spine.

Sorry. Wait. Forgot something, her text comes in. Be right back. I roll my eyes. What could she have forgotten?

But as soon as I press off the flashlight and start to text back, she comes diving over the side of the laundry basket like Captain Marvel, crashing into me, but mostly into the pile of towels next to me, scaring me half to death.

"Jeez!"

"Gotcha," she says, the basket wobbling and nearly tipping over, before righting itself with the frantic shift of both our weights.

She bursts out laughing.

"Very funny," I say, helping her to push out of the Sidney-sized indent she's left in the center of the towels. I fluff them up some so whoever collects them doesn't get mad. "You know, you could injure a guy."

"More likely myself," she says. "Did you *not* see me fall out of the boat?"

I laugh now, waiting for her to settle crisscross-applesauce against the far side of the basket. "So, how's it going, my famous genius friend?" she asks, plucking a towel and propping it behind her like a pillow. "And what was the Code PO for?"

"Code PU, more like it," I say, holding my nose.

"Ha ha," she laughs, and I smile. But, suddenly, I'm overwhelmed by sadness. This may be my last conversation with Sidney Miller in my whole entire life. *Okay, dramatic.* But at least in person. And what if it is? We live a whole plane flight away from each other.

Why did the chicken wish he could stay longer aboard a stupid research ship with geeky science kids in the middle of the stupid Pacific Ocean?

"So you couldn't sleep either?" she asks, and for a second I think she's answering the question in my head. But then I realize.

"Yeah, no. Right?" I say. "I mean, that truly was crazy. Damian Jacks, CNN. Can you believe—?" I don't have to finish the sentence. She knows as well as I do, all the things that are more than hard to believe.

"A story we'll tell our grandkids, my nana says."

"You told her?"

"Of course. I tell her everything. Plus, she already saw a teaser on the news. It'll be a feature story this Sunday evening."

"Wow," I say. "And the bite-size version is already viral. With our names on it. Your *real* name. Over 200K likes on Damian Jacks's Twitter feed."

"Wow," she echoes, then a pause. "So we should feel happy," she says, but it lands like more of a question. A question I feel in my gut.

"Right. Happy."

We're both quiet for a long, long time.

"Oh, speaking of which," I finally manage, "I bought you a present." She raises her eyes to mine in the dark, our sight finally adjusted in the dim emergency lights that dot the floor and the wonky fluorescents that spill in from the corridor. "Okay, not bought, exactly. *Brought.* Something of mine. Something—" I search for words. "Oceany," I settle on.

I dig out the Jacques Cousteau bobblehead rolled in the goldfish T-shirt.

"Sharing is caring," I say, holding it out to her.

She unrolls the T-shirt and holds the bobblehead out in front of her, shaking him to make his red-beanied head bobble enthusiastically.

"Wait, did you know I collect them?" she asks.

I didn't. I had no idea.

But I'm not surprised.

"It's synchronicity," I say.

She raises her eyebrows at me. "Like literally, Jeremy. I'm not kidding. I have three so far. Albert Einstein, Nikola Tesla, and Marie Curie. But not him! Not—" She examines him, her face twisted into a question.

"It's Jacques Cousteau. French naval officer, explorer, conservationist, filmmaker, innovator, scientist, photographer, author, and researcher who studied the sea and all forms of life in water." She looks at me suspiciously. "Wikipedia," I add. "I memorized it. FYI, he died a long time ago."

She laughs now. "So many dead scientists," she says.

"Yeah," I agree. But then I think of something. Something small now, not really clear, but something that may one day mean something way bigger. "But so many new ones, too, right?" I add, perking up some. And she does too. "Don't forget that, okay? Promise, Sidney? Ever."

"Promise I won't," she says.

FOURTEEN
TOO-FAST
HOURS LATER

33.

JEREMY JB "GOODBYE, RACHEL CARSON" BARNES

And then, somehow, we're back at the Port of Seattle.

Sidney races away from the dock to her mom and dad, who are running over to hug her.

I hang back at the gangplank—which sounds way more piratey than it is. Mom and Captain Jim and Marco and Randi and Vance and Sabira and Henry are all here with me, saying goodbye to the rest of the scientists and departing SEAmester kids.

To tell you the truth, Ms. Oceania II, the chicken is working hard not to let on how sad he is.

Finally, Sidney says something, and turns and runs back to me. I knew she'd come back at least once. After all, I'm still holding Rachel Carson in my hands.

"Don't forget this," I say, handing her over in her new swanky home, the hoop suctioned to the side, the little Styrofoam basketball bobbing along the top. "Keep working on her layup, okay?" Sidney nods, and, even though it's hard to look at her and not cry, I do. But when the words come out, the best I can manage is "So I guess this is goodbye, Rachel Carson."

"She says goodbye to you, too," Sidney says, "and that she won't forget you," then she turns and walks back toward her family, away from me, in the other direction.

34.

SIDNEY MILLER

It's true that I didn't really need to tell my parents anything.

I mean, as far as they were concerned, I was a SEAmester kid.

But Jeremy's mom makes me.

But they knew anyway.

Of course.

Everyone knows.

Everyone saw the tweets, or teasers on TV.

I mean, *everyone* did.

"Megan called," my dad says. "She said she read about it online, in Hong Kong! The shot heard 'round the world."

"Probably not the best analogy," my mom tells my dad, but she hasn't stopped smiling since they met me at the dock.

My dad only once mentions the potential dangers that might have befallen me as a stowaway, with no emergency contact form, no health insurance voucher. *Did you even have your passport?*

My mom takes Route 5 back home, along the coast, where the cliff is steep, dropping off just on the other side of the guardrail to where the whitecaps are crashing over the rocks.

"You know, your goldfish made it to the science section of the *New York Times*," my mom says.

"She did?" But I say it not like a question, because of course, I know. The newspeople picked up on that part right away. There were already hashtags: #FishyStory, plus #CodePinkOctopus, and #ConsiderTheAlbatross. Cat videos might be number one on YouTube, but a goldfish named Rachel Carson who can sink foul shots, well, you just can't beat that, can you?

I squeeze the iced-tea dispenser on my lap a little tighter. "We're almost home now," I whisper.

But when I lean over and peek at her, she doesn't look nearly as happy as you'd think she would about getting back into her own fishbowl, about not having to deal with the constant rocking of the sea, not having to hide in shower stalls or laundry rooms, leaving all those friends behind.

Leaving Jeremy.

35.

JEREMY JB "HOW DO YOU MAKE AN OCTOPUS LAUGH?" BARNES

The rumble of a big ship taking off from shore is like an earthquake under your feet. Marco explained it uses so much energy just to get moving and displace all that water, which accounts for the noise. I stare down, watching its huge white wake kick up, then squint beyond us to where the shore gets smaller and smaller.

When I can barely see land at all anymore, I send Sidney a text.

CP 🐙 Alert: Important! I type.

Forgot to ask you: How do you make an octopus laugh?

And even though I don't get an answer back right away, I keep typing anyway:

You give it ten tickles.

Don't you forget any of it, ever, I tell her.

THE END

OH, WAIT, WE'RE KIDDING. ONE MORE THING . . .

THREE YEARS
FROM NOW

36.

A pretty girl with blond hair stands chatting excitedly with a still-on-the-short-side-but-less-short-than-before boy, about fifteen, whose eyes dart constantly, in between laughing with her, toward the parking lot of the Port of Seattle loading dock.

It's not that he's not paying attention to the girl, Becky Mars, because he is, for sure—they've been friends for years now, which is how she's come to join him on this mission—but he's also waiting for someone, someone important to him, a good friend he only gets to see once a year, same time each year, for one whirlwind week, out to sea.

"It was a great NCAA season, don't you think, JB?" Becky Mars asks, but whether she's actually talking to Jeremy or more trying to impress Ben Goldman is hard to tell.

"Right?" he responds anyway, and he means it. There's no animosity or jealousy in his voice. He agrees wholeheartedly and is happy to talk football or basketball as much as marine biology, any day.

In fact, he, Jeremy JB "Co-Founder and Organizer" Barnes, still finds it hard to believe he's as well versed in science as sports, but it's true. So much so that he is the host of an annual worldwide summit of young people, now in its third year, this year promising to be the biggest and best attended, thanks in part to a recent large monetary gift from none other than Damian Jacks of CNN.

Speak of the devil. The CNN truck arrives, at the same exact moment as Nana's still-kicking pumpkin-orange Subaru.

Leave it to Sidney to time it like that.

"Hey, JB, where do you want this?"

He whips his head to look behind him, where his other best friend, Nick, the summit's new treasurer and VP, has unfurled a large white banner with a shark and a goldfish and a plastic bottle with a large red X across it on one side and a large pink sea creature on the other. Printed across its center is:

WELCOME TO THE CODE PINK OCTOPUS

3RD ANNUAL SUMMIT TO CLEAN UP OUR OCEANS

WHERE KIDS ARE THE SEA CHANGE

The last two trips, the girl's nana came on board. She rode shotgun in the inflatables, the very same seat where her granddaughter had face-planted into six feet of water not so long ago. After dinner, in the mess, Nana played folk songs on her ukulele and taught everybody the words.

"Tikkun olam," she said, putting her instrument down. "Repairing the world."

She rode with the rest of the participants—all under eighteen (except for the crew and staff)—to the spot where miles and miles of plastic bottles, couch cushions, and toothbrushes, plus millions of tiny colorful microbeads still float like unwelcome confetti and bleached bones. At least the patch was getting smaller.

Part of the solution had begun at the very first summit, with the giant sea vacuum Dr. Barnes and crew had begun to install. But more and more answers and possibilities were arriving every year, and now they were arriving via the kids.

All the original SEAmester kids—except Ashley Sperber and Chunbo Cheng, who had other commitments—had returned for the first-ever Code Pink Octopus Summit, which was held one year to the day after the boy and the girl (and the goldfish) had bid their farewells at the Port of Seattle that first year. It took a ton of planning and research, of course, but they had lots of help: you'd be surprised how a busy Twitter feed and some friends in the media can help organize things.

Also joining the group was the *real* Alex Mylanakos, a quick-witted high school senior who had missed the first trip due to chicken pox and had already been accepted into MIT for the following year.

But it was Diamond Blue who learned about, tracked down, met, and invited on board the young scientist who had discovered a bacteria that could literally eat plastic and turn it into water. Between the vacuum and the bacteria, and two or three other exciting possibilities still in the works, the Great Pacific Garbage Patch was actually shrinking.

Megan, who would be flying in from Hong Kong for the first time to attend with her best friend, Sidney (now known to all as Sidney Miller—or better yet, by those closest to her, affectionately and jokingly referred to as "Dr. Sidney Miller"), had designed the logo and all the banners and flyers.

As for Rachel Carson herself, she had been gifted, by an anonymous donor, an unbreakable fiberglass travel tank with handle that could be easily transported, replete with real freshwater aquarium plants and natural gravel. Her original mini hoop and Styrofoam basketball were placed back inside, because Rachel Carson loved them, and over time, she was only getting better at her foul shots.

What was new, however, was the addition of Louis Leakey to the tank. If you don't know who Louis Leakey is, you should look him up.

"Hey, Barnes! I'm talking to you," a kid holding the banner calls out again. "You want to give me some direction here?"

"I dunno, ask Marco," JB says, then quickly realizes: no Marco and Randi this year—the two are off snorkeling in Costa Rica on their honeymoon. Sabira and Henry are the senior mentors for this year's trip. "I mean Sabira," he corrects. "Try her. She always knows what to do around here."

And that is true. Sabira does know. As for JB, well, sometimes he does, and sometimes he doesn't know. Sometimes he's just the same old clueless funny kid he was three years ago, when he first stood on the deck of the *Oceania II* and lamented how his heart had been stomped to smithereens.

But that was a long time ago. His mother was right. Being out to sea can heal lots of things. He's never told her that. He doesn't need to. All you have to do is glance across the deck of the *Oceania II* on any given day—or across their kitchen table at home during the off-season—to see her laughing and holding hands with Captain Jim.

And then, in a heartbeat, he's off and running toward the ticket office door, which has swung wide open into the loading dock sunshine, his arms outstretched and a smile planted broadly across his face.

She's here!

So he's got some goldfish to greet, and a doctor-in-the-making, also known as his good, good friend, to hurry up and welcome aboard.

AND NOW,
THE END.

OKAY, FINE.
THE
BEGINNING.

A NOTE FROM THE AUTHORS

This book is a work of fiction, as well as a labor of love, collaboration, and synchronicity.

The inspiration came about one morning when both of us happened to be listening to the same NPR podcast about the Great Pacific Garbage Patch and one of us called the other, blathering about how we might have an idea for a new book.

Like many people, when we first set out to write it, we didn't know much about ocean science, research ships, or the Great PGP. We had both conjured up a similar image of a semisolid pile made of plastic bottles and other debris floating in the middle of the ocean. One you could walk on, like an island. In fact, our first thought was to have our characters living on it.

There were JB and Sidney, in our minds, living atop a giant mountain of garbage!

Soon enough into our research, however, we learned the Great PGP isn't like that at all—not a mound but what some call a trail or area of garbage "smog." Some of it is totally visible, like the stuff JB and Sidney observe, but even more of it—too much of it—is not visible to the naked eye and spreads way beyond the several systems of ocean currents (or gyres) scientists have logged in and studied.

The more we learned, the more we wanted to be part of a movement to make sure others knew about it, too. So we hunkered down to do what we do: Write a story that might make others care as well.

However, we knew something else right away: As is common in Jewish tradition, we believe a lesson taught with humor is a lesson retained, so we wanted to find a fun—even downright comedic—way to share this story about one of the most critical issues facing our global community today. As always, we sought out peer-reviewed articles and reputable science journals, watched documentaries, and spoke to scientists and educators who vetted the story, including those who had, actually, spent time aboard a research ship.

Having said that, this is a work of fiction and the master we serve is story. To this end, we ask for your understanding and awareness that some of the science and technical logistics in this book might not be fully accurate. There are many reasons for this. For starters, environmental science changes constantly. A giant sea vacuum, which was an exciting innovation for potentially cleaning the ocean's plastic when we began writing this book, is now looking more and more like another dashed hope. Plastic-eating enzymes and bacteria do exist, but the jury is still out on how much they can actually help.

And while we did study maps and check average or possible speeds and distances from ship to port to island to patch over and over again, in the end, the *Oceania II* is a fictional ship, and we wrote this from land, taking liberties to allow our ship to sail and stop when and where it needed to *for story.*

Cleaning the world's oceans is one scary proposition, but it's important we learn about it, talk about it, and keep pressing for ways to build awareness and take action. It's important that our young people step up with both energy and innovation.

The good news is that you and other kids, tweens, and teens like you—who, unlike our fictional heroes, are very, very real—are already stepping up to lead the way every day.

Of course, we don't recommend you stow away on a research ship, but we do encourage you to spend a semester aboard one if the opportunity presents itself, and we salute you and thank you for taking action.

You fill our world with hope.

We hope we've filled yours with some, too.

For further reading and some organizations that do amazing work to help clean up our oceans, visit:

5 Gyres Institute (5gyres.org): This group works tirelessly with local, regional, and national organizations and individuals to ban microplastics in skincare products and cosmetics in the US. This consultant to the UN and conductor of research helps people better understand the plastic crisis.

Bye Bye Plastic Bags (byebyeplasticbags.org): This group has helped change behavior and policy locally and worldwide toward the reduction or complete ban of single-use plastic bags.

College of Earth, Ocean, and Atmospheric Sciences (ceoas.oregonstate.edu): This group is known for its ocean research and exploration programs and for helping further our understanding of climate change, outreach, and education.

Environmental Defense Fund (edf.org): This group's broad mission relies on science to tackle some of today's biggest environmental battles, including overharvesting in the oceans, climate change, habitat loss, and sustainable energy.

The Nature Conservancy (nature.org/en-us): This group conducts research, advocates, and helps create environmental policy worldwide.

Ocean Conservancy (oceanconservancy.org): This group hosts coastal cleanup around the world. To get involved or run a cleanup at your own favorite beach, check the International Coastal Cleanup near you.

Plastic Pollution Coalition (plasticpollutioncoalition .org): This group's signature program, the Last Plastic Straw, presents alternatives to plastics and helps promote clean beaches, while changing commercial and consumer policy and behavior so less plastic will find its way into our oceans.

Schmidt Ocean Institute (schmidtocean.org): A private, nonprofit operating foundation established to advance oceanographic research, discovery, and knowledge, and catalyze sharing of information about the oceans. You may take a virtual tour of a research ship on their beautiful and interactive site! (https://schmidtocean.org/tour-rv-falkor)

School of Marine and Atmospheric Sciences (somas .stonybrook.edu): This research institution is dedicated to helping solve local as well as global marine science problems and making our watery world a better place.

Scripps Institution of Oceanography (scripps.ucsd .edu): Although one of the oldest and largest ocean research facilities in the world, it remains ahead of the curve when it comes to helping solve the global environmental troubles of today.

Surfrider Foundation (surfrider.org): Their mission includes fighting to reduce marine plastics. Local chapters host individual projects.

Woods Hole Oceanographic Institution (whoi.edu): This group has merged groundbreaking science with public education. Their free educational materials showcase how incredibly diverse the world of ocean research is. They offer free virtual series with scientists who bring their work alive.

With a huge thank you to Ly Williams, NYS Master Teacher of Marine Biology, and Carl LoBue, NY Ocean Programs Director, Nature Conservancy, who supplied us with this list!

Waves of gratitude to the following:

Jim McCarthy and Katelyn Detweiler, who saw the potential in a literary comedy/farce on a serious subject and helped it get a deal.

Julia Sooy, who grasped what we were trying to do even before we fully could, and then righted the ship and made it sail.

Rachel Murray, our wonderful and astute editor, who plunged in with love, insight, patience, and understanding as if it were her beloved bouncing baby from the start.

Mallory Grigg and Maike Plenzke, for the wonderful art that fully captures both the seriousness and fun of our story, and for working so hard with us to get it exactly right.

Lelia Mander, Jie Yang, Cynthia Lliguichuzhca, Lili Qian, and of course, our captain and publisher, Laura Godwin.

Karen Romano Young, for the hours she spent on the phone, sharing the spectacular photos of her time aboard the research vessel *Atlantis*, and all her insights into life on board.

Kimberly Williams, for her invaluable read and vetting of the marine science.

LuAnn O'Hair, for loving Sidney and JB from the get-go,

and, more important, for putting the early manuscript into the hands of her seventh-grade readers at Forgan Public School in Oklahoma, and especially to the one student who recommended that someone please, please, please fall overboard.

Essay, Anna Conway, and, of course, Gae's mom, Ginger Polisner, for their astute reads and wonderful feedback.